the Sinners of St Benedicts Book 3

Men & Monsters

ALSO BY ELIZABETH STEVENS

unvamped
Netherfield Prep
the Trouble with Hate is…
Accidentally Perfect
Keeping Up Appearances
Love, Lust & Friendship
Valiant Valerie
Being Not Good
The Stand-In
Popped
Safety in the Friendzone
the Art of Breaking Up
the Roommate Mistake

No More Maybes Books
No More Maybes
Gray's Blade

Royal Misadventures
Now Presenting
Lady in Training
Three of a Kind
Some Proposal
Royally Unprepared
Royals in Dating
Wishing You a Merry Misadventure

Pithy Pooka Shorts
the Romeo + Juliet Experiment

Heaven & Hell Chronicles
Damned if I do
Damned if I don't
Damned if I know

The Sinners of St Benedicts Book 3

Men & Monsters

ELIZABETH STEVENS WRITING AS

E.J. KNOX

Kinky Siren
an imprint of Sleeping Dragon Books

Men & Monsters
by E.J. Knox

Paperback ISBN: **978-1925928402**
Digital ISBN: 978-1925928396

Cover art by: Izzie Duffield

Copyright 2023 Elizabeth Stevens

Worldwide Electronic & Digital Rights
Worldwide English Language Print Rights

To letting go and moving on,
Neither of which I'll be doing with these characters just yet.

Contents

Author's Note

This is a dark, angsty, contemporary high school enemies-to-lovers romance with enough steam to melt your screen. Do not engage in public consumption unless your poker face is impenetrable.

Do not read if you don't like broken alpha males claiming what's theirs, a feisty heroine determined to break the bonds of an unwanted future, or complicated love triangles full of passion and dirty words.

This story features the heroine in sexual situations with both love interests. While not considered cheating by the characters, you may have different feelings (and that's okay). Proceed with caution.

This book is written using Australian English. This will affect the spelling, grammar and syntax you may be used to. It might come across as typos, awkward sentences, poor grammar, or missed/wrong words. In the majority of cases (I won't claim it's infallible, despite all best efforts), this is intentional and just an Aussie way of speaking (it took my US beta readers a bit to get used to). I can't say 'the' Aussie way, since we seem to differ even within the same state. Just think of us as a weird mix of British and US vernacular and colloquialisms, but with our own randomness thrown in. I still hope you enjoy it, though!

Chapter One

I smoothed out my skirts for what felt like the hundredth time in the space of a few minutes. A nervous action, my hands needing something to do like that was going to still the noise inside my head.

Apollo reached over from his seat beside me and took that hand, giving it a reassuring squeeze. "We'll be like an hour," he said softly.

I nodded. "Of course."

"We need to have a conversation with Lincoln," Archer said from the middle of the limo. I doubted he'd heard his son, but the timing was convenient, nonetheless.

Apollo nodded, but he wasn't agreeing. "Lady Wilcox expects Harlow and I front and centre."

Archer smiled, his eyes dropping down to the ring sitting proudly on my finger. "That she will."

My eyes darted to Valen, who was reclining nonchalantly at the other end of the car, behind the driver. From his position, he made no indication that he'd heard Apollo's words. I took a moment to rake my gaze over his body. Tailored dark grey suit. Black shirt, no tie, with the top button undone. Polished black shoes. His hair hung over his forehead, and he didn't bother raking it back. His phone was in his hands, and he was frowning at it as he typed on it. But then, it's not like he smiled all that often really.

As though he could feel my eyes on him, he lifted them through his hair. With Archer and Apollo busy in conversation about the rules and expectations for Lady Wilcox's party, Valen spared me a quick wink. I saw the corner of his lip twitch, as though he dared not risk any more obvious a smile. I bit my lip against a smile of my own and turned to look out of the window.

"Valk, I need you to keep an eye on the Nicolas' boys tonight," Archer said suddenly.

"Fine," was Valen's answer.

I forced myself to not look towards them. We women looked the other way when we saw too much after all. I couldn't say I hated doing it in these situations because it meant the men kept talking. Whether Archer thought I was too vapid to be paying attention or legitimately thought so little of me that he didn't think it mattered, I didn't really care to find out. Perhaps he, like Apollo and Valen, knew the women listened but also knew we wouldn't speak of it with anyone because we never did.

My eyes slid over to Frenella, who was also looking out the window as though lost in her own thoughts. Her face was neutral, the very definition of vapid. I wondered if she wasn't talking to me from the fear that even us paying attention to our surroundings enough to hold a conversation between us might be misconstrued as us *not* looking the other way.

"I expect your brother to be in position before we get there," Archer told him.

His words sent a chill of fear run down my spine and I couldn't help meeting Valen's eyes. He let his pass over me vaguely, but I could see there was reassurance in them.

"Neo's in place," was his answer.

"Good."

Cillian was in the front with the driver. Whatever Archer thought was going down that night, he was expecting trouble if he'd hired three Kincaids. And that was only if Neo didn't have anyone else with him. Neo could have his own band of people behind him for all I knew.

I turned back to the window, just in case I risked looking too interested in their conversation. I felt Apollo give my hand another squeeze, but his attention was, for all intents and purposes, on his father as they went over whatever it was they needed to talk to this Lincoln about. I didn't bother paying attention after I heard it was something about a business deal gone south. Archer was either making himself more enemies or he was crushing ones he already had. Either way, it made no difference to me.

Eventually, the limo pulled up to the swanky townhouse that the Wilcoxes used for all their fancy parties. It had been a few years since I'd been expected to be at one, but Lady Wilcox had insisted when she heard about the ring on my finger.

"An unofficial engagement party, why not," she'd said on the phone to Frenella.

I knew what it said about the 'unofficial' status that my parents hadn't gone out of their way to come as well; what that told our world about the Wilcoxes' party. But Dad had told Lord Wilcox that he had other business to attend, and we would have a proper party after the school year ended. He knew as well as I that hopefully the whole charade would be done by then, but we had to keep up appearances on all fronts if we wanted a chance to minimise casualties.

Valen climbed out first, holding the door as he helped Frenella out. I saw Cillian standing behind him, already surveying as though on alert for danger. A thrill of trepidation ran through me, and I wondered what Archer anticipated happening at the Wilcoxes' party of all places. More like, what the hell had Archer done now to be concerned about retaliation?

My turn to leave the limo was next and I did the whole demure slide/shuffle to the door, taking Valen's proffered hand to steady me and aid my graceful exit. Cillian cleared his throat and my eyes darted to him quickly. His eyes widened almost imperceptibly, and I couldn't stop mine rolling at him; if he thought this wasn't normal behaviour then he had a lot to learn about normal behaviour. His eyebrow rose and I saw the smirk deep behind his eyes.

I inclined my head to Valen in thanks as I extricated my hand – not too quickly, not too slowly – before going to stand with Frenella. She took my arm in hers and we made our way to the front door where Lady Wilcox was waiting to greet us as any good, nosey host was wont to do.

"Harlow Vanguard," she said warmly, and I saw the shrewdness in her eyes. "It's been too long, dear."

I mean, she could have invited me to any number of soirees over the years and just hadn't, but sure. I forced my sweetest smile. "Lady Wilcox. That is has. It's a pleasure to be here tonight."

She made a 'tsk' sound and waved her hand dismissively. "Nonsense. You are our guests of honour. Being the first ones to celebrate the union between the Callahan and Vanguard families. I almost didn't have time to organise the cake."

Jesus. There was going to be cake?

Well, I supposed I may as well enjoy it. All going well, this would be the only engagement party Apollo and I had. As much as I was committed to Valen and the future we had fallen into maybe a bit earlier than we'd have done it otherwise, I'd spent so much of my life pretending to have another one that it was sort of nice to get to pretend now. Like this could be a goodbye to that part of my life before moving on with one I chose for myself.

I made my smile wider. "You spoil us."

Lady Wilcox almost nodded but stopped herself just in time. "Anything for the Vanguards."

I hadn't realised that Archer was behind me, but I was fairly sure that was him stiffening in annoyance. Knowing what I did now, that didn't come as a surprise. The contract between our fathers was clearly not common knowledge among the rest of our world, and he had to keep his plans for world domination to himself. I still didn't really understand why it was okay if Apollo and I married naturally – for, like, love and all – but not if it was contracted. The men had thrown around the whole 'Law of Legions' thing, but never really explained it in detail. I assumed it was, like many things, just one of those things that would start to make sense in time.

"I'll let you get in and we'll have a proper catch up later," Lady Wilcox said. "I'd like to hear all about the wedding."

I'd been prepared to have a million questions directed at me about the wedding. This was, after all, our first official outing after our 'engagement'. But I was eighteen! How quickly did they expect me to get married? Let alone start planning every minute detail?

Oh, yeah.

I was a woman in our world.

I was supposed to have spent my whole life planning my wedding. The ring on my finger was supposed to just be the sign that I got to start putting all that theoretical planning into practice. That ring was a sign I had achieved the highest possible achievement for a person like me; someone was taking me off my family's hands and would both provide for me and breed me to further their agenda.

How silly of me to have forgotten. To actually want my own life.

Which was an annoying mentality to be walking into the Wilcoxes' party with, because the number of people whose first question to me was wedding-related was…every one of them. No 'hello' or 'how are you?', just a question about the wedding. Were all the women actually as vapid as our world expected them to be? Or was this the façade in full effect? Did these people have nothing better to do with their lives than speculate over when these teenagers were going to be married and start pumping out heirs?

As though he could read my mood, Apollo swung me onto the dancefloor. All I had for him was gratitude.

"Thank you," I told him quietly.

He smirked. "I could feel you tensing up."

I shook my head. "I'm sorry. I…was all up in my head as we walked in, and every question just makes me angrier."

Apollo's smile for me was genuine, warm. Like nothing had changed from a year ago when we were playing this very thing as nothing more than friends. "Don't apologise. They're a bunch of nosey, old fuckers whose lives are so interminably boring that they have nothing better to do than gossip about our wedding. It's ridiculous."

Hearing it from Apollo's mouth, I went into defensive mode. "They are what our world made them," I reminded him, and he had the decency to look chastened. "Like us, they're playing their role. Besides, we're engaged, of course they expect we're excited. It's not like we have to save money for the wedding or get our lives established so we can live or anything. We're both eighteen. So, why wouldn't we get married straight away?"

He nodded. "No, I guess not." We danced in silence for a few moments until Apollo dipped his lips to my ear. "Valk wanted me to tell you that he loves you."

I smiled as though his words had been sweet nothings that warmed my heart. "If he thinks that's going to fulfil today's quota, he's sorely mistaken."

"I *think*," Apollo corrected me, "he thinks that's going to stop him punching me in front of all the toffs for putting my hands on you all night."

That sounded more likely. "And how do you think that's going for him?"

We both snuck a look over to where Valen was lounging against a wall. He was half-shadowed, but I'd had him committed to memory long enough to fill in the blanks. Arms crossed across his broad chest. One leg crossed at his ankle and the mother of all murderous looks on his gorgeous face.

"I think he'll be fine waiting until we get home."

I tried not to smile and encourage his shit-stirring. I knew it couldn't be easy on Valen. It wasn't easy on me when I'd rather be in Valen's arms in front of everyone else, being able to talk to him about my anger, to find comfort in him. But we had to do what we had to do.

Apollo and I went about our night. Talking to anyone and everyone, being paraded around by Lady Wilcox while she proudly exclaimed how wonderful we looked together. As usual, Apollo kept a hand on me at all times. Small touches that had become so ingrained in our relationship that, even now, they were still second nature. Like we were still an extension of each other. It made pretending easier. It made keeping my eyes of Valen easier.

At some point, Valen appeared beside us, his eyes darting around as though there was a threat lurking in every shadow.

"Time to go," Valen said quietly.

Apollo nodded once. "Which way?"

"We need to split. You're coming with me. Harlow's—"

"You take Harlow," Apollo said, looking between us in panic.

Valen shook his head. "People will notice that's not protocol. Don't worry, I've found a…decent replacement."

"Apollo. Harlow."

The voice sounded very Eastern European. I turned and saw it belonged to a woman who could only have been Valen's sister. Even if I hadn't heard about a sister, the similarities would have been too uncanny. Long near-black hair with a thick fringe, and grey eyes just like her brother. She was almost as tall as him as well, in a slim black jumpsuit with a plunging neckline. Beside me, I could practically feel Apollo's eyes pop out of his sockets at the sight of her.

"Valentina," Valen said by way of introduction.

"Creative naming there," Apollo remarked, though his voice sounded a little tight, and Valen growled.

"Not now," he snapped.

Valentina smirked. "*Otets* was very disappointed to find out I was not a son."

Valen, I noticed, was avoiding looking at me. His eyes were firmly focussed on the room around us, and he would only let them fall over his sister or Apollo.

"We'll meet you back at the estate," he said to Valentina.

She inclined her head. "*Da*. We will see you there."

"Marco will meet you outside. And don't get too chatty," he said softly, a clear warning.

Valentina's eyes shone so much that they were almost silver. "I promise nothing, little brother."

Apollo snorted and Valen shot him a warning look. Apollo held his hands up in defence.

"Shall we?" he asked and Valen nodded.

Valentina's hand went to my back, and she led me out a side door. I recognised Marco's car waiting for us and he nodded to me from the driver's seat. Valentina opened the back door for me, and I climbed in. She waved me over to the other seat and got in after me.

"Where's Neo?" Marco asked casually.

Valentina shrugged. "Valen thought it would be dangerous to put us in a car together."

Marco snorted. "Things going that well for you, then? Maybe you need to just fuck each other and get over it." Before she could reply, Marco started the car. "Righto, buckle up, then, ladies. O'Malley Luxury Chauffeur Services is ready for take-off."

"I think you have mixed your...*metafory*." Valentina frowned, but I wasn't sure if it was because of the quip about Neo or because she was looking for the right word.

"Metaphors?" I suggested and she smiled at me.

"*Da*. Metaphors. *Spasibo*." She looked me over calculatingly as Marco pulled away from the building. "My brother speaks little of you."

I inclined my head. "I'm not surprised. He doesn't really speak in general."

I heard Marco fail to cover a laugh in the front seat. Valentina noticed.

"I am jealous of the two of you," she said simply as she sat back in her seat. "Who have spent these years with him when our families saw fit to keep us apart."

"Oh, if you'd lived them with Valk, you'd certainly be changing your tune," Marco offered.

"Perhaps. But at least you had the option available to you."

"If it makes you feel better," I said. "Valen and I hated each other until..." I paused. "Actually, I'm not sure when we stopped really."

Marco scoffed good-naturedly. "Ye and Valk never rightly hated each other, missus," he reminded me. "Ye both wanted what ye thought ye couldn't have."

I looked at him pointedly and Valentina huffed, "If you think I do not know what you are to him, then you are mistaken."

"He told you?"

She smirked and she was gorgeous. "*Otets* told his mother, who told our *babushka*. Those two never could keep a secret. Babushka thought it might be prudent for one of the family to check in on the little wolf cub and see if he could benefit from *semeynaya podderzhka*." Another frown. "Support of the family."

I nodded. "I'm sure he would rather die than actually show you how much it means to him."

"Is that his policy with you, Miss Vanguard?" she asked.

"Harlow, please, Valentina."

"Valya."

"Valya. And, yes, pretty much."

"He nearly did. Aye, missus?" Marco added from the front. "He needed more'n a few pretty tricks to beat Peskov."

Valya looked between us. "*Dedushka* could not decide if he was proud of Valen or wanted to wage war for that."

"If it helps," Marco said as my phone vibrated. "Valk was trying very hard to pretend he wasn't totally in love with our Miss Vanguard here. There is nothing quite like a good beating to aid in one's denial. Not that we could assuage Cillian or Mr Callahan with that excuse."

My phone vibrated as I wondered how heavily Cillian and Archer needed *assuaging*, and I pulled it out of my pocket.

Valen

Safe?

If it wasn't the man of few words himself.

Harlow

Not too chatty, if that's your

concern.

"I'm not sure it does help," Valya said. "But then I would not pass up the chance to beat up Peskov either."

I smiled and decided then that I could quite like Valya. She was so very much like Valen – there must have been a lot of nature in them – but she was clearly more open, more talkative, not afraid to be human. Or funny. I wondered if there would be a chance to get to know her better before all this was over. And hope that we weren't on opposing sides when it was.

Chapter Two

The trip back to the Callahan estate was uneventful for everyone. While I appreciated it, I also really wanted to know what the threat was for it to be so anticlimactic. There wasn't even a debrief for the Kincaids.

As we walked inside, I did notice Neo and Valya arguing about something quietly between each other, but I didn't pay it much mind as I knew I was about to finally be allowed to have some time with Valen.

Valen, who preceded Apollo and I up the stairs as Archer disappeared into his study and Frenella headed for the salon for her pre-bed cup of tea.

"Good night, you three," Frenella called to us.

"Night, Mum."

"Good night, Frenella."

"Night, Mrs Callahan."

At the top of the stairs, it was just the three of us. With no one to see, Apollo's hand dropped from mine as my other reached for Valen's. It twitched like he was going to pull it away, then he gripped me tightly.

"I suppose I'll see you two in the morning?" Apollo said

cheekily.

Valen whirled on him, his hand falling from mine again, and shoved him into the wall. "You want to be lucky you're going to *see* morning, mate," he snarled.

Apollo smirked. "Is this about that one slip?" There may have been an incident with Apollo's hand and my arse.

Valen growled. "If that was a 'slip', I'm a fucking nun."

"I'm just keeping up the ruse, Valk."

"You watch what you touch, *God*."

Apollo nodded, his eyes going colder. "It would be a shame if anyone was to guess that my relationship with Harlow was anything but sincere, wouldn't it, *Morningstar*?"

Valen's eye twitched over the new moniker. "It wouldn't be the first time the two of you had a tiff."

"It also wouldn't be the first time we were faking, but we managed it the first time." Apollo shrugged. "Just trust me to know what needs doing."

Valen blinked but rallied. "Like I was supposed to trust you last time? When that ring on her finger meant something and you fucked around anyway?"

"And what about you?" Apollo drew himself up. "You didn't fuck up at all, did you, Mister Golden Boy? Or now you're all tame, should I call you Golden *Retriever*?"

Valen met him, their chests up close together. "I gave her up for you," he snarled. "You gave her up for some fucking Magdalen."

Despite the turn the conversation was taking, I knew better by now than to get between them when they were like this. Whatever this was, whatever they were getting out of it, they needed it. Needed to work out their frustrations. It was how they worked. They didn't bottle up their issues. If they needed to throw fists over something, they would. If fists weren't needed, then words would suffice. Not letting them argue would only make things worse.

Apollo's face twisted in a grimace. "I'm not proud of what I did, Valk. But you won the day, so I'd think you'd be a little more grateful for the lengths I'm going to for you."

Valen shoved against him. "You want me to be grateful? You've got everything you wanted; Daddy's approval *and* getting to fuck whoever you want."

"Oh, and you *don't* have everything you want?" Apollo pointed to me.

"Not when I have to sneak around just to be with the woman I love–"

"Like that stopped the two of you before."

Valen shoved him again. "Not when being with her risks all-out war among the Nameless. No one has pulled something like this in the whole history of the Company. There's the Law of Legions. There're all the broken contracts someone has to collect on. We put one fucking foot wrong and we're all dead. *Harlow's* dead. So, no, mate. I don't have everything I want. But you not inciting me to hit you for putting your hands where they don't belong is a fucking good start."

Apollo looked like he was thinking a few choice things, but he only nodded. "Fine. Fine." He held up those hands. "I will be more careful where I put my hands in future."

Valen nodded as well. "Good."

"Good."

They gave each other a short hug, then sniffed like the show of emotion was a little too much for either of them.

Apollo inclined his head to me. "Night, Harlow."

I smiled at him. "Night, Apollo."

Apollo looked to Valen once more, they both nodded at each other again, then Apollo disappeared into his room and Valen was storming to his. I was going to ask them what they expected me to do, but I knew Valen wasn't in the mood for too much sass, so I just followed him to find him pulling his jacket off.

"Is it time you reminded me who I belong to?" I asked him as I closed the door with my body, sliding my tongue over my lip as I locked it behind me.

His eyes darted to me as he ripped his shirt off his arms. It was unnecessarily sexy, even if he was epically pissed off. "Are you done playing the part of doting fiancée and now it's time for the help to fuck you like you need, princess?" he growled.

"Oh, are you jealous, love?" I teased him as I pushed off the door and went to him.

He was not in the teasing mood as he stared down at me through his hair, fury in his eyes. "More than I should be considering we all know where we stand now. It's not like it was before, love. When you were his and I was just lucky to pretend you were mine when I could have you. Now, you're mine but I still have to watch him touch you and make you smile while I can do nothing."

I ran my hand over his cheek. "You do everything," I told him softly and I saw some of his anger melt away. "I *am* yours, Valen. And you are mine. Nothing can come between us now."

He leant his head to mine as he closed his eyes. "I love your optimism, love. But we still have a long way to go."

I took his face in my hands and waited until he was looking into my eyes again. "We have nothing but time, love," I whispered as I ran my nose over his. "Would you rather the Nameless let us be together in peace, or do you want to go to war with the whole fucking world just to call me yours?"

He wrapped his arm around me and pulled me tight to his body. "I would go to war with the world for you in a heartbeat, love. But peace will be easier." It was a begrudging admission.

I nodded. "Peace will be easier. And for peace, we need to be patient."

"I am not a patient man, princess."

I bit my lip as I looked into those grey eyes. "Oh, I know."

The heat in those eyes was reaching a dangerous level. "And I have waited to be with you for long enough."

"Then what are you waiting for, Valen? I'm right here, very ready for you to do *whatever* you want to me."

He ran his tongue so very slowly over his lip. "Do not test me, Princess."

I leant into him. "Do you need to be reminded where you belong, Valk?"

His grip on me tightened. "Do you?" he growled, his voice low and gravelly and stirring the need deep inside me.

I gave him a single nod. "I think I do," I whispered.

He crushed his lips to mine as his fingers made swift work of practically ripping my dress off me. He pulled away for a split second to look me over in my bra, panties and heels and I heard the appreciative rumble in his chest. Then he spun me and pressed me up against the wall. One hand held my wrists against the wall above my head and the other worshipped me. It was hot across my skin, but it wasn't enough. My nipples were tight, my clit throbbed. I needed him closer. So. Much. Closer.

I bucked my hips against him in silent plea and I felt his smile against my cheek where his head rested over my shoulder. "Do ye need something, love?" he murmured as his fingers dropped to the waistband of my panties. One ran over the band, hooking in at my hip bone making a tingle zing around my whole body. My breath came shorter, and his smile widened. "Tell me what you want, Princess," he begged. "Tell me what you want me to do to you. Ask me nicely." His hand left my panties and slipped up my body to wrap gently around my throat. He turned my face to look at him and purred, "Beg me."

I was at his utter mercy, and I loved every second of it. "Make me scream your name, Valen. Make me cum. Make sure I never forget the feel of you. Do not stop until you've given me every ounce of pleasure my body can handle. Understood?"

His answer was more feral growl than words. "Understood."

He kissed my neck as he pressed me closer to the wall. His hand left my throat and slid down my body, this time not stopping until his finger dipped inside me. My whole body reacted, melting against him and I moaned in pleasure.

He pumped me hard, his thumb finding my clit, and it didn't take long for the climax to wash over me one. Twice. Without giving me a moment to recover – with no complaints from me – his hand left me, and I felt him undoing his trousers behind me.

Valen slammed into me. His right hand slid over the top of my thigh agonisingly slowly, gripping me tightly and using it for more leverage. As his left hand dropped down to knead my breast, he groaned my name in my ear and everything in me tingled and fluttered.

"Does the big, bad wolf like that?" I asked him and I felt him nod as he pressed his face to my shoulder.

"You'll be the death of me, love," he breathed before he slid out of me and spun me around.

He picked me up and carried me to the bed, kissing me hard. He dropped me gently and I watched, enraptured, as he stripped off his trousers and boxer-briefs. He went slowly, like it was a show, and I relished every single second of it. He licked his lip as he reached down and yanked my panties off me before crawling over me and sliding back in. My knee hugged his hip tightly and my head fell back as his lips went to my neck again.

As my next orgasm crashed over me, my nails dug into his shoulders and my back arched off the bed. I felt his smile, then he was pulling out and those lips were trailing kisses and gentle nips down my body until he was between my legs.

The stubble across Valen's jaw grazed the inside of my thighs and it was so damned sexy. My hand tightened in his hair as my back arched off the bed and I whimpered, low and needy.

"I've barely touched you, love," he chuckled, oh so roughly, nipping the skin of my leg playfully.

I smiled to myself. "I've missed you."

He shook his head, his lips trailing over me as his hands tightened on me. "That's not all."

"I'm not telling you," I said. "It's embarrassing."

He looked up at me quickly then, in one smooth motion, he sat up and pulled me down the bed so his head hovered over mine. "What's embarrassing, princess?"

I bit my lip and shook my head. It only served to make him frown harder.

"Nothing about us should be embarrassing, Harlow." Shit. I'd pissed him off by making it seem like there was a problem when there really wasn't one.

I chewed on my lip now as I looked into those grey eyes. I took his cheek in my hand. "It's your stubble," I told him carefully.

That surprised him. "If you want me to shave, I'll shave. I've just been too lazy."

"You've been busy. I know."

He pressed a quick kiss to my lips. "I'll do it now." He made to pull away and I held him fast. Understandably, confusion swam in his eyes.

I shook my head. "No, love. Please don't."

The confusion gave way to a heated humour as he searched my eyes. The corner of his lips tipped sinfully. "Does the good little princess like it?"

I gave him a single nod. "I like it very much."

His smirk grew as his slid his hand firmly up the outside of my leg. "What do you like about it, love?"

"There's open and honest communication with trust and love, and then there's you baiting something out of me just so you can tease me."

He dropped his lips to my neck. "All right. How's this? Every time you put your hands in my hair, especially when you pull on it, it makes my fucking stomach drop, my heart jump and my cock twitch. I love the way you drag your teeth over my ear. The feeling of your nails in my skin as I fuck you makes me nearly nut myself right there. And every single fucking time you moan my name when you cum, I fall more and more in love with you." He pulled back only far enough to look into my eyes. His eyes soft and reverent. "Your turn."

Okay. I could do this. Valen did it, so of course I could do it. After all, he was supposed to be the one with the emotional range of a pebble. I took a breath and told myself it wasn't embarrassing when it was sincere.

"I don't know why, but it's so sexy when your stubble grazes my skin. The heat it leaves behind turns me on so much. The stark colour contrast on your jaw makes your eyes more silver than grey, and there's something about the whole package that speaks to something… I don't know. Like, primal in me. I look at you and want to drag you to my cave and never let you leave."

"How very Neanderthal of you, love," he joked as he gripped my hips tightly.

"And that." I forced a deep breath as I nodded. "I… When you touch me, so strong and sure and steady, at that point just before that decadent pain, my whole body tingles."

He leant forward and dragged his teeth over my neck. I sank back onto the bed, and he came with me.

"Shit, Valen…" I groaned.

"What else do you like, Princess?"

"God, everything. Hard. Fast. Frantic, when it makes me feel like you can't control yourself around me. Like I drive you even half as mad as you drive me."

He huffed a rough laugh as he lifted my knee and slid into

me. "I'm quite sure you drive me far wilder than I drive you," he said.

I clawed at his back as mine arched off the bed. "The great Valen Kincaid, known for having the control of a monk?"

Another spluttered laugh. "Control of a monk? I couldn't resist you. That night in the woods… I used up every single ounce of control I had not to have you right there. By the time I found you in the rec room the next week, I had no hope. I resigned myself then to the fact I could be a dead man. But I wanted you and, for some reason I was too desperate to question, you wanted me, too."

"I never knew you felt that way about me," I said softly, hugging him closer as he thrust into me slow and steady.

"That, love, was the fucking point." I heard the humour in his voice.

"Did you know?"

"Know what? How badly I wanted you? It was *very* hard – if you catch my drift – to miss."

I smiled. "No. That I felt the same."

He shook his head and grazed his lips over my neck. "No. No fucking clue. You blindsided me, princess. You were the first person to truly surprise me. In so many ways."

I ran my fingers through his hair as we rocked together. "I love you."

He looked into my eyes and said, "I love you," before kissing me deeply.

Chapter Three

As the three of us hung out in the rec room the next day before heading back to school, my phone vibrated. I looked at it to see Dad was calling.

"I'll get the door," Apollo said, jumping up.

I nodded to him as I answered the phone. "Hey, Dad."

"Harlow," was his answer.

"What's up?"

"I'm negotiating a meeting with Cillian."

I looked to Valen, who cocked his head in question. I put the phone on speaker so the boys could listen in as well.

"And it's not going well, to put it mildly," Dad continued. "In all honesty, the idea of an exclusive contract with the Kincaids is attractive. No one in their right mind wouldn't find it an attractive business proposition. And our family is very willing to pay the price."

"Being me," I clarified and Valen smirked.

"Being you," Dad agreed. "I just have to convince Cillian that the price is worth it."

"I'm well aware how little the Kincaids think of women–"

"It's not just that," Dad interrupted. "We have to tread

carefully. Cillian will need to be given all the information about the contract we're trying to replace and why if he's got any hope of agreeing."

"Da can keep the secret," Valen said.

Dad didn't say anything for a moment. "Valen."

"Rex."

"I am well-versed in negotiating with Brawn, son. I know how tight-lipped you lot can be. I wouldn't be surprised if, between you, you had enough ammunition on the Brains to stage an epic coup."

"What are the Brawn and the Brains?" I asked, feeling stupid.

"Ruling families are the Brains," Dad offered.

"Those who protect them are the Brawn."

"Those who do the rest are the Grunts," Apollo said, coming back from the door. "Hey, Rex."

"Apollo. What are the three of you up to, then?"

"Nothing I'm sure you're thinking," Apollo said with a laugh and Valen glared at him. "Just lazing around until we leave for school."

"How were the Wilcoxes?" Dad asked.

"Insufferable," was Apollo's answer.

"We didn't stay long," I added. "I don't think Lady Wilcox was pleased."

"Maybe Archer shouldn't be stirring up trouble with the Nicholas Boys, then," Valen huffed.

"First the Rossanos and now the Nicholases?" Dad sighed, then muttered, "Fucking hell, Archer."

"With about ten Kincaids on site, we were fine," I told him.

"We got them out before there was a chance to not be fine," Valen growled.

"I hear your sister is visiting, Valk," Dad said pointedly.

"Aye, she is," Valen said carefully.

"Make sure she comes to the negotiations."

"Da would have to put her six feet deep for her to miss it," Valen promised.

"Good. Harlow could use some more women in the room."

"Sorry," I interjected, looking around. "I'm going as well?"

"Of course, you are," Dad said. "This is your contract, Harlow. If we want the Nameless to take you seriously as my heir, then you need to be at the forefront of all negotiations. We have to show the Council that no one makes decisions for you."

"Are they going to be okay with that?" I asked.

Dad gave a dry laugh. "No. Of course, not. They're going to fight us and argue the whole way. But it's what we have to do."

"How much danger does this put you in? All of you?" I asked.

"A lot," Dad answered. "Until we have the Council's approval for this contract, we're open to any number of bounties on our heads."

My stomach tried plummeting out of my arse. Both Valen and Apollo must have noticed.

"But," Apollo said. "Once it's settled, and everything's signed, then we're good. Dad shouldn't be able to touch us with raining down the full might of the whole Company and the Council."

"Shouldn't?" I said, not liking the ambiguity in that word.

Valen shrugged. "Our moral code is…fluid."

"The one thing we have going for us is that no one on the Council knows about the contract between Archer and I," Dad said. "It's not common knowledge among the Nameless. Certainly not the extent."

"The rest of the fuckers think it's a standard marriage contract," Valen offered, sounding very much like that's what he'd thought for a very long time. I wondered when Apollo had put him right. "Outside of the four of us and Archer, the O'Malleys are the only ones who know the truth." Valen glared at Apollo as though letting him know how pissed off he was to find out after Marco.

"So we get the contract, and we take it and the evidence to the Council and hope they rule in our favour?" I asked.

"That is our only way forward."

"What does Cillian think the meeting is about?" Apollo asked. "Have you given him the details?"

"I've impressed upon him my interest in a new contract between Harlow and Valen of a matrimonial nature. I've left it up to him to guess about the circumstances and my motives."

"We've spoken…" Valen said hesitantly. "A bit. He asked me if I'd be interested in a marriage contract with the Vanguards. I had to walk a fine line between disinterested and keen to make sure he didn't pass it up. I must have misjudged my level of interest, because Nana Kincaid reached out East for aid."

"So, he guesses there's more to it?" Dad asked.

"If he does, he hasn't said. More likely, he told Nana what happened, and she guesses there's more to it. I've…avoided her since."

Dad sighed like he wasn't sure if that made things better or worse for our cause. "All right. And what about the Black Bloods? Any news?"

Because of course Dad had found out about Florence and me being kidnapped by the Black Bloods. I assumed that was Marco's doing, but he had neither confirmed nor denied his involvement.

"So far, all quiet," Valen reported. "But Harlow is never without one of the Angels off school grounds."

"And even then, I'm only allowed any privacy in my dorm room," I added.

"Precautions must be taken," Dad said sternly, and I knew he was going to brook no argument from me about my 'protection'.

"There is one complication," Valen said, as though he was loathe to bring it up.

"And what is that?" Dad's voice was hard.

"Kane has joined the Black Bloods."

My blood froze and I was pretty sure my heart stopped. "What?" I breathed.

Valen nodded, thinking my reaction to his brother's name was the same as usual. "I only found out this week. Idiot probably thinks he can rise up their ranks and it'll make him feel better about how shit he is."

I actually stumbled backwards.

"Harlow?" Apollo said and Valen's eyes lurched to me.

"What is it?" Dad asked.

I shook my head. "Neo said I couldn't tell. Marco said–"

"Couldn't tell what?" Valen snarled.

I took a deep breath and forced myself to meet his eyes. "Over Christmas… When you were gone. Kane was here with Neo. He found me and…" My eyes closed for a moment as I tried to keep down the bile rising in my throat. "He tried to… Neo stopped him, but we both knew… We both knew that Kane would take the next chance he had, and he wouldn't hesitate."

"That was two fucking months ago and you never said anything?" Valen said, his voice too calm. Eerily calm. Like a storm was about to break above us, calm.

"When did Kane join the Black Bloods?" Dad asked.

Valen nodded. "You think it's connected."

"Are you saying you don't?"

"Hang on," Apollo said, holding his hand up. "You think Kane joined the Black Bloods so he could use them to get to Harlow?"

I had to sit down. It was the conclusion my head was coming to, but I hadn't wanted to make that final connection.

"I think Kane either plans or already has taken them over so he can get to Harlow," Valen said.

"Why, though?" Dad asked.

Both Apollo and Valen looked at me.

It was no surprise that Valen recognised Kane's interest in me. He'd made comments that, in hindsight, made perfect sense. It was me who, at the time, hadn't realised exactly why Kane looked at me the way he did or how far he was willing to take it. But I hadn't thought Apollo had noticed.

It was him who answered Dad, as though Valen didn't trust himself to speak. "Kane's has his eye on Harlow since the day Dad signed the contract with Cillian to make Valk my first

Angel.

"He's obsessed with her," Valen said, his voice shaking.

"And no one thought to tell me?" Dad was clearly not impressed with the younger generation taking matters into their own hands.

"I didn't realise it was a problem until now." Equally, Valen was not impressed with some of taking matters into our own hands.

"Neo said that even for the sake of fulfilling a contract, killing your own blood was a messy business. He and Marco told me not to tell you."

Apollo's eyes went wide. "That's why he turned up early?"

I nodded. "Neo sent for him."

"Neo knew about Marco as well?"

I shrugged. "I guess."

Valen scrubbed a hand over his face. "How the fuck does he know *everything*?" he sighed, like there were more secrets Neo knew that maybe he shouldn't.

I remembered Neo's cryptic words the day Kane attacked me. "Does he know about us?"

Valen nodded. "I think so. He hasn't rightly said, but…"

"Convincing Neo may be easier than convincing Cillian," Dad mused out loud.

"You propose killing the head of Family Kincaid?" Apollo scoffed.

"No. I propose winning over the heir to the Family Kincaid so he can help us convince his father."

"It could work, but we have to tread lightly," Valen said.

"Why?" Dad asked, obviously thinking that the more

information we had, the better.

"Valentina…" He paused, looking exasperated. "My sister is a staunch advocate of the contract. She and Neo have…"

Apollo laughed, "It's been a fucking week and they're already at each other's throats."

Valen's eyebrows jumped. "It's not the throat I think they want at."

"As fascinating as this glimpse into your family life is, Valk," Dad said. "How do you propose we proceed?"

"Leave Neo to me. I can…bring him around as long as Valentina doesn't interfere too much. You work on getting the meeting with my da. Let us know when it is, and we'll be there."

"Said as though your father won't make you be there already. And Apollo?" Dad clarified. "Because Cillian will need to know we have you on side."

"I wouldn't miss it," Apollo promised. "Anything to make this work."

I gave him an appreciative smile.

"Good," Dad said. "Good. All right. Well, I'll let you lot get back to school and give you any more updates as I have them. But Valk…"

"Yes, Rex?"

"The next time my daughter's life is under threat; I expect to be kept informed. We are all on the same side, son. Let's keep it that way."

"Yes, Rex," Valen answered.

"Goodbye, Harlow. We'll speak soon."

"Bye, Dad. Love you."

"Love you, too."

After he'd hung up, there was a very pregnant silence hovering between us all.

"You're angry," I said to Valen.

He nodded. "Livid might be a more accurate description, love."

"Yeah, I'm not exactly thrilled," Apollo added. "What were you two thinking?"

"Me and Neo, or me and Maroc?" I challenged, not liking them ganging up on me, even if I understood where the fear was coming from.

"Either," Apollo said as Valen answered, "Take your pick."

I shrugged. "I don't know. Neo seemed pretty convinced you'd kill Kane if you found out–"

"Not an incorrect assessment," Apollo pointed out and Valen growled at him to shut him up.

"And Marco backed him up on that being bad. I thought I was protecting you."

"From what?" Valen cried, throwing his arms up. "You think I couldn't take my idiot half-brother?"

"I *think* Neo made it sound like your dad would react pretty fucking badly and, as much as I'm sure you could take him in a fight as well, I didn't think you'd want to. I didn't want to put you in that position."

Valen deflated a little, but the anger still burned in him. "He deserves to die."

I nodded. "I'm not going to argue that one. Kane…creeps me out something awful. But surely the more important thing now is the contract? You can kill him once your dad's on side and the ink is dry," I told him, and he actually smiled.

"I will hold you to that, love," he vowed.

I inclined my head. "I'm okay with that."

Valen's phone rung now, but it was clearly not a call that concerned the lot of us as he answered in Scots and headed out.

I looked at the time on my phone. "I guess I need to finish sorting my shit before we leave," I told Apollo, who nodded somewhat awkwardly. I gave him a smile and headed to my room.

"Harlow?" Apollo said and I turned back to him with a quizzical expression.

"Yeah?"

"Uh… Not great timing, but I don't know how to say this other than to just say it but… You should know I… Well, I fucked– Slept–" He winced. "Had sex with Florence."

Of all the things I thought he might have said to me, that was definitely not it. I also didn't expect him to stumble over word choice. I blinked, trying to wrap my head around that. I couldn't say I didn't know how it could possibly have happened. After all, Valen and I happened. I was just surprised I hadn't noticed anything.

But who he slept with wasn't my business, even if I was burning to beg Floss for a debrief the same way we debriefed after pretty much all our encounters. But she hadn't been the one to tell me, Apollo had, so I'd have to wait and see if she'd be ready to tell me as well.

I gave him a nod. "Thanks for telling me."

He chewed his lip. "You're not mad?"

Weirdly, I wasn't mad. What Apollo got up to in his own time was on him. I thought it was kind of weird that the two of them had ended up in bed – or not – together. But I also wasn't. I remembered all those times I'd thought I knew them better than for their chemistry to be unresolved sexual tension. I realised now how naïve I'd been. Or rather, how stupid I'd been. I was sure it had been borne of my own tensions with Valen projecting onto my best friends; I hadn't wanted to see anything more between Florence and Apollo because then maybe someone could see the more between Valen and I.

I shook my head. "I'm not mad, Apollo," I promised him.

He looked pleasantly surprised. "Oh. Okay, um, cool." He paused and looked me over like he was looking for bullshit. "You're not worried I'm going to hurt her or *did* hurt her or I'm going to fuck it up or anything?"

I snorted. "Florence Walton can more than look after herself," I reminded him. "Especially with you. If she didn't put up with your shit when she thought you and I were dating, then she's not going to put up with your shit just because you fucked her."

He grinned. "No, I suppose not."

"I mean, if you hurt her, I *will* hurt you, of course."

He inclined his head. "Of course."

"But I'm not worried about it."

He smiled. "Okay, then."

I tapped his arm awkwardly. "But seriously–"

"Don't hurt her?"

Now I smiled. "Well, yeah. But I was going to say, really, thank you for telling me. It means a lot."

He shrugged. "I'm trying this whole honesty thing. Maybe it won't make me a new man, but I know I fucked up royally with us and…I'm trying."

"Just make sure you sort your shit before you actually fall in love with someone, yeah?"

He huffed a laugh, but there wasn't a lot of humour in it. "Yeah. I will. Promise. I'm sorry, Harlow. Again."

I nodded. "Me, too. Not that it's anyone's fault, but I'm still sorry that I couldn't be what you needed."

"You are exactly what I needed. I just need to work on knowing the difference between actual love and just lust mixed with intense connection from shared history."

I gave him a smile and pulled him into a hug. "You'll get there. We'll all get there, Apollo."

He nodded as he buried his face in my shoulder. "I know. I know."

I squeezed him tighter, then felt his squeeze go tense. Pulling back, I saw his eyes were behind me. I turned and saw Valen in the doorway, paused like he wasn't sure if he was interrupting something or not.

"You almost ready to go?" I asked, letting go of Apollo. "I think I have a couple more things to pack up, then I'm good."

Valen nodded slowly, his eyes still on Apollo as I walked past him. I reached up and he lowered his cheek to let me kiss it. I patted his chest and went to my room to finish getting organised and leave them to whatever they needed to sort out now.

Chapter Four

The weather was finally warming up. Slowly. With about four weeks until Easter, it was about damn time. The early mornings and late evenings were still cold as hell, but the midday sun had the propensity to actually provide some nice warmth.

Florence and I were making some good use of the afternoon as we took our slow time heading nowhere particular after choir practice. We were arm in arm and walking like idiots, swinging one foot in front of each other's as we went.

"If I'd known how early you'd have to deal with the Council, I'd have mentioned them earlier," she told me.

"Earlier?"

She nodded. "It didn't seem relevant to anyone at the time. It was just useless knowledge I had. But I guess I didn't expect our lives to get so exciting," she chuckled.

"You've known about the Nameless this whole time?" I asked her, incredulous.

I'd stupidly – naïvely? – assumed that Florence had only found out about them when I had. That it was something we'd uncovered together, both as ignorant about the real working of our world as each other and now I find out, it was just me? Not that any of that was Florence's fault.

She shrugged. "Of course, I did. My father is their accountant and I'm a sneaky bitch. Like the whole shebang. Council. Affiliates. He balances the books for every transaction that occurs in the Company."

I blinked, not sure where I was going to start with all my questions. "So, the contact between Dad and Archer…?"

She shook her head. "Alas., I did some snooping of my own last holidays, and he knows nothing, which confirms their contract is outside the Nameless."

I sighed, knowing it was pointless to ask her what kind of snooping. Like she said, she was a sneaky bitch, and her information would be valid. "I don't know enough about all this."

"I told Apollo. For whatever that's worth. I figured God and his Angels would know what to do with the info, although it didn't seem like anything new."

I looked at her quickly. "Did you? When?"

She shrugged again, far more nonchalant than before. "Oh, uh. When you and Valen were… One time… I guess…"

Clearly, she still wasn't ready to say anything about her and Apollo and that was fine. I wasn't going to rush her into telling me anything she didn't want to. I was still burning to know if she wasn't telling me because it meant too much, or not enough.

So, I just nodded and said, "Fair enough," and changed the subject.

When we made our way to dinner that night, Ryko smirked as he saw Florence and I approaching. He was the supposed next in line for top Angel when Apollo handed the title onto Tyson at the end of the year. He fully expected that he'd be the next Valen, and he had the ego to match.

"Here she comes," he said as we sat down. "The woman with the golden pussy who's tamed not one Angel, but also the Wolf."

I felt Florence stiffen next to me, but she turned a winning smile on him. "Jealousy is a very unattractive colour on you, Ryko," she told him.

As Ryko gave a piss poor imitation of a howl, Valen walked up behind him.

"You done?" Valen growled before grabbing the back of Ryko's shirt and hauling him off his seat. "I think you owe Miss Walton an apology, Shitling."

Ryko glared at us, and I bit my lip against a smile, knowing that that was not going to get him n Valen's good books.

"I said apologise." Valen's voice dropped even lower.

"She's not even one of us," was Ryko's very inadequate defence.

I stood, planting my hands on the table. "Apologise," I demanded.

Ryko looked me over like he was planning to disagree. I might have been the official Goddess of Saint Benedicts now, but there were plenty of Saintlings who were still averse to listening to a woman, regardless of her status.

I glared at him harder. "Apologise, Ryko."

His lips rippled in a snarl. "My apologies, Miss Walton," he ground out, then added quickly, "that I don't give a fuck how good your–"

Valen spun him around and one-punched him to the floor. The rest of the Saintlings all looked at him in abject surprise as he just stepped over Ryko's unconscious form and took his seat at the table and nodded to one of the smaller ones to get him something to eat while throwing what was left of Ryko's dinner at another one.

Florence gave him a nod, knowing what ruse she was supposed to be playing as well as I did. She didn't have to pretend to be dating Valen, but they had agreed that she would be his alibi. Because in the history of Valen's time at Saint Benedicts, there had never been a time when he'd abstained this long from fucking around and there had to be scapegoat that wasn't me. Because it would get suspicious if Valen wasn't fucking around and he spent all his time with me and Apollo. It would be less suspicious if he wasn't fucking around and he was spending all his time with me, Apollo *and* Florence.

Not that it made it easy on any of us, and I knew that. So I brought it up with Floss when we got back to our room.

"So?" I hedged. "How is it being the one who's tamed the big, bad wolf?"

Florence sighed. "Less fun that I expected."

I nodded. "You mean the fact everyone's saying you're making your way through the Angel ranks?"

She looked at me with a 'what do you think?'. "No. It's the fact that everyone asks me if we want a threesome," she said sarcastically.

"It's the fact that–"

She nodded. "It's the fact everyone thinks I'm making my way through all the Angels. You know, the Magdalens actually worship me now."

I laughed. "Really?"

She smiled. "Really. Something about the fact that neither Marco nor Valen have been known to fuck anyone else while partaking of my gorgeous pussy." She indicated to it and everything.

I snorted. "Oh, Jesus."

"Yep. Not only that, but Marco tried faking a fight with Valk over me today in aid of the rumour."

"I'll bet that went well for Marco."

"Valk's actual fury was enough for Marco to call intimidation and get off with a minor black eye."

I sighed heavily. "I didn't think this was going to be easy," I said carefully.

"But you didn't think it was going to be this hard?"

I shook my head. "I didn't think it was going to negatively impact the people I love quite so much."

"Listen to me, sister," she said firmly. "What you and Valk have is worth a few rumours about my sexual prowess."

"You're not actually hating this are you?"

"I don't hate it, no. Is it going to make things difficult if I ever actually fall for someone? Yeah, probably. But we'll cross that bridge when – nay, if – we come to it."

"Hopefully it's a sweet and innocent Frenchman by the name of Jean-Luc with a fondness for charcoal sketching who has no idea who the Nameless are."

"As long as he fucks me dirty, that sounds ideal."

We looked at each other for a second, then burst into laughter.

As our laughter died, Florence nodded to my desk. "Are you going over more of the contracts tonight?"

I looked to my computer as well and took a deep breath. "I need to be ready to meet Cillian," I answered. "If I don't know them backwards and inside out, then there is no way I can walk in there and hold my own."

She nodded. "Do you need any help?"

I shrugged. "I honestly don't know." I pulled my hair back. "You've got to get ready for your next retreat anyway, don't you?"

She waved her hand at me. "I've got time to help my best friend prevent war."

I snorted. "Jesus, it sounds so dramatic when you put it like that. Like, what are we? In some dystopian novel?"

She chuckled. "I guess our world is kind dystopian when you think about it."

I nodded. "Yeah, true. Look, I'll get started on this next lot, you do what you need to do for the retreat, and I'll interrupt you if I need help?"

"Sounds like a plan, babe. But Harlow…"

I looked back to her as I sat at my desk. "Mm?"

"Do ask."

I blinked. "Of course. Why wouldn't I?"

Her smile was all shit-eating. "Because you feel guilty about neglecting me lately and you think that letting me get on with retreat stuff will make it up to me."

Damn her for knowing me so well.

"What will make it up to me is letting me in, not shutting me out," she said carefully, and I nodded. "I'm serious. Even if you think you're doing it for a good reason, don't exclude me. I'd rather botch this next retreat and have to do catch up work than not be by your side for this. Even if I can't literally be by your side the whole time."

I went over to her and gave her a huge hug. One that wasn't nearly big enough for her years of support and friendship. "I promise," I told her. "No shutting you out. I'll bug you every five seconds."

Her laugh was a little watery and I realised my own eyes were a little hot. "Okay. Good."

I went back to my desk and opened the folder with all the documents Dad had been sending me over the last two weeks since I'd gone to him about not marrying Apollo. I'd been over most of them at least three times and was still trying to wrap my head around what they all meant.

It was like a crash course in some overly complicated political history, probably because that was exactly what it was. And I had five days to get it all straight in my head because, all going well, we would have our first meeting with Cillian on Sunday.

Chapter Five

"Get back into bed, love," Valen grumbled from where he was lying on his stomach, totally at home among my sheets and taking up the majority of the smaller bed.

"I'm meeting Florence," I told him.

Florence had been out the night before – I chose not to ask where in case it was Apollo – so when Valen and I had fallen into bed in my dorm room the night before, we'd just decided to stay there. She'd texted before I fell asleep saying she'd meet me at the café in the morning. Suspicious, but hopefully in a good way.

"Do not put those on," he warned me as I picked up my panties.

"Valen," I laughed.

He lifted his head and levelled as serious a stare on me as he could while still half asleep. "You will not like what I do to you if you put those on," he growled and fuck, but it was sexy.

I bit my lip. "On the contrary, love. I think I'll very much like what you do to me if I put them on."

He frowned and dragged his hand through his hair. "I said I'd wait until – if – you wanted proper rough, Harlow, but I'm not above giving you a taste of it if you disobey me."

He swiped his arm out to grab me, but I skipped out of his reach. He frowned deeper and growled again as he slid out of bed.

"I thought I was in charge?" I teased him.

"Are you really testing a man while he's still got raging morning wood, princess?"

I smirked. "I might be."

When he took hold of my hand, I let him pull me to him. He wrapped his arms around my waist and looked down at me with a very serious expression. "Do ye *want* me to have to punish you, princess?" he asked, and I heard the humour trying to break through his sternness.

I bit my lip as I slid my arms around his shoulders. "Oh, I think you've wanted to punish me since before my birthday, Valk."

He picked me up with a deep growl. "I think you need a shower before you leave, princess. Dirty girl."

I bit my lip harder to stop my laughter and nodded solemnly. "If you say so."

"I do."

He took me into the shower where very little washing occurred and even then only after Valen had wrung three orgasms out of me. He finally let me go and, thanks to me trying to get ready earlier than strictly necessary, I was only about fifteen minutes late to meet Florence.

We snagged a booth at the back of the café, which wasn't terribly busy for that early in the morning – convenient for letting Valen sneak out without anyone much noticing. But then it was made easier by the rumour that he was fucking Florence.

And speaking of fucking…

"I fucked Apollo," she burst out as soon as my arse hit the seat, and I tried to hide my smile at the sheer nervousness on her face.

"You did what?" I asked her, acting angry.

She paled. "I know. I'm sorry. I'm a terrible friend. But it meant nothing. It was a real, proper hate fuck. It just happened. Please forgive me. I love you!"

I couldn't do it anymore. I couldn't pretend I was surprised or angry. A snort escaped me, and she blinked at me.

"What?" she asked.

I gave her an apologetic look. "I know," I told her.

"You know? How do you know? Why didn't you say anything?"

I shrugged. "I figured you'd tell me at some point. Apollo told me a couple of days ago."

Florence's surprise grew. "He told you?"

I nodded. "Yeah. Why is that a shock?"

"I dunno. I guess it just… Why would he have told you?"

"I guess he learnt his lesson about lying to me? Why? What do you think it was? It meant something to him?"

Her eyes bugged as she looked at me. "Do you think it did?"

"I wasn't there. I can't answer that. Do *you* think it meant something?"

She frowned. "Don't turn this back on me like I always do to you."

I shrugged as I took a sip. "Fine. I won't. Today."

She rolled her eyes. "Fine. Tomorrow, you may begin your

dissection, Doctor Vanguard. Psych me and see if my hate fuck is actually not so secretly true love." She snorted, but I wasn't going to make the assumption it was just a joke. Not yet anyway. Not after Valen and I.

Then, I was distracted by my phone going off.

Valya

I am taking you and Valen to dinner

tonight.

"Huh," I said as I read it.

"Dick pic?" Florence asked hopefully as she snuck a look over my shoulder.

I grinned. "Valen's sister."

"Oo, the Russian. What does she want?"

"Dinner. Tonight."

"I'm totally coming, too. I want to meet her."

I smiled as I typed out a reply.

Harlow

Sounds good. Can I bring Florence,

too?

Valya

Of course. And the Callahan child,

why not. We'll make it a party.

Florence snorted and I knew she'd read the message as well. "God, I like her already."

"You think she sounds hot," I challenged.

"I have very good reason. You told me she was hot."

I nodded. "Yeah. Okay. I can't deny that. She is hot."

"But is that just because she's the girl version of Valen?"

"Oh, no," I assured her. "Not at all. She's Valya-hot, not Valen-hot."

"I cannot wait to see what Valya-hot is," Floss chuckled.

Valya sent me the information for a swanky-looking restaurant in one of the towns outside Bieityn. One of those towns we went to when we didn't want to run into anyone from school. Where, hopefully, Valen and I could just be us without worrying about prying eyes.

We were still careful as we got out of the car and headed inside, though.

"We're meeting Valentina Volkov," Apollo said as the maître d' met us.

He inclined his head. "Very good. Follow me."

Florence and I linked arms as we were led through the restaurant, towards the back.

Valen looked around suspiciously. I wasn't sure if he was looking for anyone we might know, or if he thought we were being led out the back to be shot, or something equally as dramatic.

The maître d' took us up some stairs and opened the door to a private room. It was kitted out with a bar and a private kitchen, complete with two servers, another behind the bar and three chefs.

"This is *swanky* swanky," Florence whistled to me as Valya stood up and spread her arms wide.

"Hello," she said with a smile.

Apollo was, once again, a little starstruck and I didn't much blame him. Valya wore another jumpsuit and this one showed a lot more skin than the last one. And Apollo had always been a sucker for skin.

Florence noticed and snorted. I tried not to speculate about what they were or could be based on their reactions. I tried and failed. But they seemed nothing more than the usual frenemies. Whether there were still benefits or not would remain to be seen.

"Valya," I said when no one else spoke. "This is Florence."

Florence pushed forward. "Floss."

Valya inclined her head as she wrapped Florence up in a massive hug and I was pretty sure Florence swooned a little. "It is a pleasure to meet you, Floss. I have heard only good things."

"Not from Valen, surely," Florence teased and Valya laughed.

Valen grumbled and dropped into a chair, motioning to the bar staff for a drink. We'd got Marco to drive us, so he wasn't going to have to worry about that. Even Marco had realised that Valen was going to need alcohol to get through tonight. He'd pulled me aside and not so subtly reminded me that the whole Valya thing was new and Valen didn't do 'new' very well.

Valya directed me to sit beside him, and I took the opportunity, but I watched the staff.

"They are being well paid for their silence," she assured me before she put her hand on Valen's shoulder companionably and sat back down.

Valen's eyes were on her and I wasn't sure if that was begrudging gratitude or just keen wariness in those stormy depths.

I watched the way the two of them interacted. I knew that they'd only met recently, but she looked at him like a proper doting big sister. It was clear she not only loved him, but she cared about him. She wanted the best for him. Whatever reason the Volkovs had actually sent her over, she was here with good intentions.

Around us the servers were getting drinks ready. I assumed Valya had given them directions. Or maybe it was the kind of place who liked to think they knew what you wanted.

"Now," she started as Florence and Apollo sat as well. "We have all night to talk and drink and get to know each other. I told Babushka I would make sure this Vanguard was good enough to share our blood."

I choked on the water I'd chosen to sip at that moment.

Valya laughed. "As though you have not thought about children already, no?"

I snuck a look to Valen to gauge his reaction.

Yeah, we'd talked about children. Talked about the fact that, if he'd knocked me up, he'd be a dead man. I'd then thought about it, decided I liked the idea for some reason, but known it was never happening. Now there was a very real chance of it happening. I was pretty sure I knew what I wanted, but what did he want?

"There's no rush," Valen said as he picked up the tumbler of caramel-coloured liquid he'd been given.

"Maybe, but do you not want to?" she pressed, and I think he surprised the whole table when he nodded so confidently as he took a sip.

"You do?" I blurted out.

"Have you not spoken together?" Valya asked, picking up her own glass.

Valen's eyes darted to me. "We're not exactly in a position to do much of anything right now," he reminded his sister. "Whether we're ready or not."

"You are negotiating a marriage contract and you have not discussed the children."

"We've barely begun the negotiations," I told her. "Are we supposed to have planned the wedding already as well?"

She leant on the table towards me. "Why not? You want to marry him, yes?"

I nodded. "Of course. But this contract is necessity as much as desire. It's been less than two weeks. How much could we have planned in that time?"

"Everything. If you'd wanted to."

"Valentina," Valen muttered as he threw back the rest of his glass.

She shrugged and I appreciated how unapologetic she was. "What? She professes to want to marry you and yet how has she proven herself good enough for my little brother?"

"It's not Harlow who has to prove herself," Valen said as he motioned for another drink.

"You are a Volkov–"

"Fucking hell!" Valen exploded. "You promised you'd behave. It's the only reason I fucking agreed to this. We have enough shit to deal with from the rest of the world without the people in this room piling on!"

I slid my hand into his and gave it a squeeze. He tipped his head back, closed his eyes and groaned in frustration before taking a deep breath.

"Personally, I think that's your proof," Florence said and Valya smiled at her with a cheeky wink. Florence tried to hide a smirk.

Valen grunted again and looked back at us. "I'm going to need the bottle and I'm going to need my women to agree to a fucking truce."

"Your women?" Valya laughed as she grinned at me. "I think he just made us family, Harlow."

I gave his hand another squeeze and I returned her smile. "I've never had a sister."

"Oh, you are lucky," Valya said. "I grew up with five. It was the brothers we were missing."

"You didn't miss much," I assured her, pointing at Apollo. "If this one was anything to go by."

"I wasn't that bad," Apollo said.

"Not that bad? Dude, you were constantly farting on me!"

He laughed and even Florence wrinkled her nose in a combination of disgust and amusement.

"There were worse brothers," Valen said, his eyes on Apollo through his hair.

"And I have asked you to let me kill him," was Valya's response.

Valen rolled his eyes and poured another drink. "It's life. You want me to kill your sisters for taking too long in the bathroom in the morning and stealing your lipgloss?"

"He put you in a coff–"

"There was an air hose!" Valen hissed, like they'd had this

conversation a hundred times. "I don't even know why she told you."

I looked between them, caught between wanting to know what had happened to Valen and knowing there was a lot he didn't tell me, and more I probably didn't really want to know.

"You know, there was one time at the Callahan estate that Apollo and I tried making a tree house," I started, hoping to cover the awkwardness. Apollo clearly remembered as he snorted Whiskey out of his nose. I laughed. "I fell out and broke my arm."

"Yeah, and I tried saving you like some dashing knight and got a fucking concussion," Apollo finished.

"What about the time you set the towels on fire in the bathroom?" Florence suggested.

I nodded. "There was that time."

"How do you start a fire in a bathroom?" Valya asked.

"I was having a spa day," I said pointedly.

"You were being an idiot," Valen muttered.

I flushed as I remembered.

"There is a story there," Valya realised.

I couldn't help smiling. "It was winter break, and we were all at the Callahan Estate. What was it? Three years ago? Floss had given me these really nice candles for my birthday. I wasn't going to use them and waste them, but she made me promise I would. So there I was, lit candles all over the bathroom and I go and knock one off the side of the bath right onto one of Frenella's best towels. Fire ensues, I scream and Valen comes running in to find me butt naked, covered in bubbles and flapping over this tiny fire."

There was a small smile on Valen's face that he tried hiding in his glass.

"He yells at me," I continued as he squeezed my hand. "Calls me an idiot—"

"A fucking idiot," he clarified.

I nodded. "A fucking idiot. And he storms into the room, all ready to deal with my little fire, and I've dripped water everywhere, so he slips over and his arse lands right on the fire."

"Ye're lucky I didn't go up in flames," Valen said softly.

"Why didn't I know about this?" Apollo huffed a laugh.

I shrugged. "Uh, I don't know. We didn't tell you?"

He shook his head as he looked between us.

I knew why I hadn't told him. I hadn't told him because what happened next was that I freaked out and fell over. And I didn't just fall over, I fell into Valen's lap. I'd been soaped up and naked in Valen's lap three years ago and we'd both known, even then, that Apollo could never know. I wouldn't have been able to talk about it without blushing like mad and giving away exactly what I'd felt. Looking back, maybe Valen's reasons had been pretty similar after all.

"Tell me, Harlow," Valya said, her turn to break the awkwardness. "What is your plan for meeting with my father on Sunday?" Although, her choice of topic was an interesting one. At least it was something we could all talk about without – hopefully – any of the weirdness we'd fallen into with the previous ones.

Chapter Six

Marco pulled up to the hotel, hopping out of the car to open my door. Apollo helped himself out and looked up at the building.

"What are you doing?" I teased him. "Looking for threats?"

"Hot tip," Marco joined in. "Anyone up there would have dealt with us. Look up when you're still in the car, immediate vicinity before getting out, then further afield once she's out."

I looked between them. "Was that actual advice?"

Marco shrugged it off. "Does it hurt?"

I kept the full plethora of my thoughts to myself. "I guess not."

"Come on," Marco said, ushering me inside. "I want this over with as soon as possible."

"Nervous about seeing Cillian Kincaid in person?" I joked.

"Shitting myself about being stuck in a room with Cillian, Neo, Valen and Valentina Kincaid in person," he clarified, not at all embarrassed about his admission. "On the flip side, having Apollo, you and your dad at my back is not exactly filling me with the undeserved confidence I am so used to."

"We're not going to have to fight our way out," I told him.

He inclined his head like he was prepared for otherwise but

said no more.

As we walked towards the elevator, I saw Dad was waiting for us in the lobby. He fell into step with us, all business-like.

"It's good to see you in person, Harlow," Dad said, giving my hand a small squeeze as we waited for the elevator.

I nodded. "You, too."

"Next break, come home and we'll get started on what you need to know."

"My internship?" I teased and he smiled.

"Your internship."

I nodded. "Sounds good."

He touched my hand again and his eyes darted behind us for a moment. "Make sure Marco comes, too. The boy needs to earn his retainer."

"Just how large *is* his retainer?" I asked, looking to Marco myself.

Dad's smirk grew rueful, as did Marco's. "Large enough that he's finally starting to earn it."

"I do me best," Marco added.

"And how many figures is that?" I asked as the doors opened.

Dad put his hand behind me to indicate I preceded him into the elevator. "I'll take you over all the books at Easter."

I would have to be happy enough with that for now. "Okay, then."

The four of us headed for the designated room. Neo was standing outside to let us in. I noticed the holster under his jacket, and I wondered what he and Marco – at least – were expecting to happen here. Then again, Dad had told me about plenty of negotiations that had resulted in multiple deaths in the middle of signing. And those were the ones that had been considered a relative success.

"Vanguard," came the booming, thick Scottish accent of Cillian Kincaid. He was sitting on a couch that faced another.

Behind him, Valya and Valen stood looking like twins with their dour expressions. Then Valya winked at me, and I tried to hide my answering smile.

"Cillian," was Dad's answer.

"Tell me exactly what you're offering here, Vanguard," Cillian said.

Dad took one step back and inclined his head towards me.

"You'll be dealing with me during these negotiations, Cillian," I informed him as I sat on the opposite couch. Dad, Marco and Apollo took up position behind me much the same way as Valen, Valya and Neo stood behind Cillian.

He looked me over like he wasn't convinced. "Then get on with it."

I inclined my head. "Fine. In exchange for an exclusive contract with the Kincaids, the Vanguard Family offer you my hand in marriage and the full financial backing of the Vanguard Empire. All agreements therein would only hold for the term of the marriage, whether dissolution occurs through divorce or death."

Cillian scoffed, but I saw the consideration in his eyes. "An exclusive contract? Ye want to *own* the Kincaids to get out of marrying Callahan's progeny?" His eyes darted to Apollo behind me.

"I want to work with the Kincaids to be with the man I love," was my careful answer.

"Love? Ye want me to believe that ye fell in love with my son, Miss Vanguard?" Cillian said, looking at me pointedly. I felt like he knew Valen's answer to that, but my answer was what was important at this point.

I swallowed. "Yes. What? Just because you fail to love your own children, you think no one could?"

Valen's eyes weren't the only ones that widened in shock and probably concern about my immediate safety. Neo seemed quite concerned about my audacity as well. Behind their father, Valya smirked at me.

Cillian's eyes roved over me. "I see that backbone finally came in, lass. I'm almost tempted to agree to this contract just to save you the attentions of your future father-in-law when he finally works out how savvy that mind really is."

I hid my trepidation. Would Archer actually assault me? I wasn't that naïve little child anymore. I knew the answer. And the answer was; yes, he would. He wouldn't care if Apollo loved me, if he wanted me then he'd take me. Another power play. Another way to make everyone around him subordinate, even his heir.

I swallowed. "Then, why don't you?" I challenged.

"Because I'm not convinced that 'you love each other' is a good enough reason to renege on any of the Family's current contracts, Miss Vanguard. Nor to sign my family over to the whim of the Vanguards for – God willing – the next sixty- or seventy-odd years."

"Really?" I huffed, not bothering to hide my frustration because showing him I wouldn't bow to him gave me power.

"And what exactly would convince you, Cillian?"

"You are a start, lass. I'm not saying no to talking about it. I'm willing to let you convince me. But I'm not saying it'll be easy. Has your daddy given you all the information you need to know what you're asking of the Kincaids?" Him and his fucking patronisation.

Fine, I'd give him what he wanted.

I drew myself up and plastered on the perfect princess mask, complete with simpering, vapid smile and hands clasped in front of my stomach. "I realise you don't know me very well, Cillian." My voice was calm, gentle and demure. "But I am nothing if not prepared. I have been over every single one of the contracts between our three families in the last one hundred years from the Nameless archives. I have noted how they affect the truces, alliances and relations both between us and our wider associates. If you think I misunderstand the seriousness of what I'm asking of you, then you are very mistaken, and I suggest that you reevaluate who you think you're negotiating with. I will do whatever it takes to be with Valen, but I would rather you and I come to the agreement amicably." I forced my smile wider and batted my eyes at him.

Cillian's mouth had dropped open a touch and his eyes were blinking rapidly before he pulled himself together. With the majority of the room facing away from him, Valen pointedly rearranged the bulge in his trousers as he looked at me. Neo's face was a stony as usual, but I saw a hint of warmth in his blue eyes. And Valya. Well, she had no qualms about telling me just what she thought of my speech; she fucking applauded me.

"Valentina," Cillian snapped.

"*Otets*," she chuckled. "I think our Harlow gives even Nana Kincaid a run for her money, *da*?"

"*Da*," Cillian said absently, then shook his head. "Aye, she does." Then he amended as he directed his words to me. "You do, lass. Ye play the game far better than many women I've met in the Company. I'm starting to believe that you will make a fine wife for my boy, but that doesna change the fact that Kincaids aren't known for marrying or that entering into this contract risks war."

"The reason we are asking for this contract is to avoid war, Cillian," I reminded him sharply. "And what is it about Valen marrying that you're against? Is it him wanting something you have avoided? Or perhaps something that has avoided you?"

Cillian's lip tipped and I saw where Valen had inherited the smirk that he'd perfected. "I appreciate your fire, lass. But I need more'n pretty words from a pretty face to sign my whole family over to yours for the life of your marriage."

I was going to let the comment about my pretty face pass. For now. "What more? Money? Heirs? Soldiers? What could possibly convince you?"

"Mostly, lass, time. Time to work out how my affairs would look on the other side of this contract and whether I'd be happy with that appearance. But I wouldn't say no to heirs or soldiers. Tell me, do you plan to finish school before you start pumping them out, or will ye get started right away?"

I didn't rise to the bait. "I applaud your attempt to shock me," I told him, deadpan, because it was honestly a bit pathetic at this point. "Providing it is possible for me to bear Valen's children, I think that's our business."

His eyes darted behind me. "Is it? And how about the Callahan boy? How many of 'my' heirs will have his blood?"

My body scooted forward, my hand shot out of its own accord, and I smacked him across the face. For the space of one heartbeat, I panicked. As I sat back, I regretted my hasty action and was absolutely terrified about the retribution that was coming my way. Then I realised that, "Fuck you, Cillian Kincaid."

He grinned as he turned his face back to mine. "Good," was his answer. "But I had to be sure."

"Sure that I wasn't a little whore?" I spat. "Why the fuck would I be doing all this just to keep Apollo on the side? That is senseless." I wasn't going to look back to Apollo at this point, but Valen sure looked at him, and I could feel Apollo's presence burning against the hairs on the nape of my neck.

"As senseless as it seems for a Vanguard to be negotiating a marriage contract with a Kincaid. There has never been a single marriage contract for a Kincaid in the whole Family's history—"

"I do so love the way you discount the long line of women who have sacrificed so much for your 'Family'."

Cillian had the decency to look somewhat chastened, but his jaw was tight. "It is better little girls do not speak of things they do not know."

I hardened my own expression. "It is better that old men do not make assumptions based on the fact I keep my sexual organs on the inside."

He inclined his head towards me. "Aye, perhaps it is."

"You agreed to meet, Cillian. If you wanted more time, what

did you hope to expect from today?" I asked him.

"I needed to see for myself how serious this was. I wanted to know what you were willing to offer. Phone calls and emails are sure convenient, but nothing beats an old-fashioned meet up, lass. It tells one so much about the other party."

"And what did it tell you about me?"

"Enough. You and your da send us your draft contract and we'll go from there. Every stipulation and clause. I'm not promising anything, but I see no reason to see if we can't both benefit from a new situation."

I think I managed to hide just how relieved I was to hear him say that. I inclined my head to him in thanks. "We will."

"Then I propose we all have a drink and conclude our business for today."

The whole room seemed to breathe a sigh of relief, Marco being the most notable. Valen went to him and Apollo, their three heads bowed in discussion. Dad and Cillian went to the drinks trolley, but I noticed that Neo and Valya were also wrapped in a conversation of their own. And it looked heated.

Everything I'd heard so far about Valya and Neo was one hundred percent confirmed. The tension between them was legitimately thick enough to cut. I wasn't sure how much of it was hate and how much was lust – or a potent mix of the two – but I sure knew about that particular predicament.

Was that what Valen and I had looked like at the beginning of the year? Or was I just seeing the potential for love in everyone's hate because I'd found my own? Because I understood how fine that line was, how easy it was to hate when love seemed so far out of reach, so impossible, something that belonged to other people.

Chapter Seven

I checked my phone again. On seeing no new notifications, I dropped it back onto my stomach and sighed way more loudly than necessary. Apollo laughed.

"Fuck, you are actually mooning."

I glared at him as I sat up. "I'm not mooning."

He nodded. "You're mooning. I never imagined you'd been a mooner." He fake gasped. "Did you moon over me?"

I turned a pointed look on him now. "That is a very dangerous question, Apollo."

His grin turned sheepish. "Yeah, I guess so…"

I felt like honesty might be good for us here. "Depending on your definition of mooning, I spent the better part of my life mooning over you, *God.*"

"You did?"

I huffed a laugh. Of course, he was still fucking oblivious. I shook my head as I rearranged and settled in. "I waited for you, Apollo. I waited to be your friend. I waited to be your girlfriend. I waited to be your fiancée. I waited to be a priority. And…I'm never entirely sure I was ever even one of those things to you."

"You're my best friend, Harlow."

I nodded. "The princess is your best friend. The girl who was waiting. The girl you were supposed to marry." I fiddled with the ring on my finger. "But I'm not sure you were ever mine."

"Harlow, I love you. I love Valen, too, but I don't have the same relationship with him that I have with you. I can't talk to him about my feelings or my fears."

"Have you tried?"

"We say what's necessary and that's fine. I have you."

I forced a smile and nodded. "I'm glad I can be there for you."

"Fuck," he muttered. "That's what you were talking about, isn't it?"

I huffed a laugh, and there was a bit of humour in it. "Yeah, Apollo. That's kind of what I was talking about."

He shook his head. "I'm trying, Harlow."

I took his hand and rubbed it. "I know. I can see that. I don't expect you to be Mr Perfect Sensitivity overnight. It's been less than a month."

"Then talk to me."

"About what?"

"Whatever you like. I want to know. I want to listen."

I nodded. "All right. Can I ask you something?" My fingers went to Valen's cross at my throat, and Apollo's eyes followed them.

"Ah..." he said.

I nodded. "I wore it for months while we…" I wasn't sure how to finish that sentence. Luckily, he felt no need to either.

"And I didn't notice?"

"And you didn't notice."

He inclined his head and let out a rough sigh, "Yeah… If I've learnt anything from this whole…" He looked at me. "Well, you know." I nodded. "It's that this year has not been my finest moment."

"The whole year?" I teased.

He gave me a rueful smirk. "It's been a *very* long moment." He licked his lip like he was stalling for time. "If you asked me now to tell you what Valk's cross looked like, I only could if I was looking at it. Same with yours. I could tell you they were silver, but beyond that… I'm such a fucking arsehole." He let out another sigh, and I could tell how annoyed he was with himself.

I waited for him to continue. "I only knew Valk's was missing because it wasn't on him. It took me too long – it took me losing you – but I've realised that the man they made me might not be the man I want to be after all, Harlow. I just don't know how to be anyone else."

I took his hand and leant my head on his shoulder as we looked out over the grounds. "I think believing there's another life out there for us, that it can be in our reach, is a start."

"Is that how you felt?"

I nodded and sat up again but left my hand where it was. "I always felt like I was living someone else's life. Even when it looked like we'd work out, I was living on someone else's timeline. My life was never my own."

Knowing me so well, Apollo knew what cane next. "Until Valk."

I swallowed. "Valen…let me be me. Without masks. It

didn't matter if I didn't stay in my box with him because what we were was outside the rules. My defiance was…"

"Sexy?" Apollo offered and I felt myself smile.

"Part of the banter, the battle, the dynamic. What we were would never live in the real world, so we didn't need the charades. There was little risk that our true selves would be found out by anyone else. We would keep each other's secret, because the way we knew those secrets was a far bigger one."

"And how's that whole 'never living in the real world' thing treating you?"

"Uh…" I huffed a laugh. "Yeah, it could be better. I honestly don't know what's worse; when I wanted him so badly but fully believed I could never have him, or having him and knowing I could still lose him at any moment. Our whole relationship, we've been in limbo or purgatory. I'm terrified that we won't know how to deal if – when – we ever get out."

"What do you mean 'deal'?"

I shrugged. "You know. Like, will it even work? I love him, Apollo. I know I do, and I know he loves me. But does he *like* me? Does he know me? What if, when we finally get to date and be seen in public, to have the chance to just exist together, what if he thinks I'm boring or we have nothing to talk about? We never had that problem, me and you."

He nudged me with his shoulder. "You think it's just sex?"

"I think we haven't had a chance for it to be much more, and I'm scared we'll go through all this pain and uncertainty and maybe kill a whole bunch of people only for him to realise it was all a mistake."

Apollo scoffed and I looked at him incredulously.

"What?" I asked.

He shook his head. "No. I just… I know Valk, Harlow. He's not the kind of guy who talks to anyone unless he gets to threaten them, or he loves them. He's not going to be doing any of this – a fucking Kincaid offering himself in my place least of all – without having spent *years* agonising over it."

"Years?"

Apollo nodded. "Yeah, years. I would be willing to bet my trust fund that Valen Kincaid knew exactly how far he'd go for you before he even touched you. He might not have consciously realised he knew, but he did know what he was doing."

The way Valen and I started, I wasn't so sure. But Apollo seemed convinced that Valen had been willing to die for me from the moment he first saw me.

"What I find *more* interesting," Apollo continued, "is the fact you think he'll realise it was a mistake, but you have no such concerns about yourself?"

I sighed. "I guess I'm projecting. *I* don't know me yet, but Valen's known who he is his whole life. I'm actually looking forward to spending as long as it takes to get to know him fully, but how long will a guy who's so sure of himself love me when I'm not sure of myself at all?"

"Harlow," Apollo said gently, pulling his hand from mine only to put his arm around me. "I would not be surprised if Valk knows you better than you or I know you. Not just who you are, but he's watched you fight the bars on your cage to be you, to be with him. And he will consider it a privilege and an honour to be by your side as you keep discovering who you are and what you want to do."

My eyes got hot, and I cleared the lump from my throat.

"Are you going to cry now?" he teased, holding me tighter.

I nodded. "I might. Is that okay?"

"Happy tears or sad tears?"

I pressed my lips together. "Happy. Relieved. Nervous. But not sad."

He leant his forehead to mine. "Then, yeah. It's more than okay."

My next laugh was a little watery. "Okay, then. Good. Because I'm not sure I can stop it."

"You never have to with me, Harlow," he said warmly. "I've done a pretty shitty job until now, but I'm here for you. However you need me. I mean, I'll fart on you if you think that will help?"

I snorted. There were tears and snot and it was disgusting, but Apollo just laughed his damned head off.

"I think I've had enough of your gas to last me a lifetime, but thanks," I said.

He shrugged. "Okay, but my offer stands."

Which was good, because over the next two weeks, I needed him. Him and Florence. Valen was constantly disappearing. I saw him less than I had at the start of the year. He was no longer always hovering. He was barely in class, he wasn't at meals in the dining hall, and when he finally fell into bed beside me, he was asleep as soon as his head hit the pillow, whether he was still wearing his boots or not.

"I think I'm forgetting what his face looks like," Apollo said, trying to ease the tension.

We were sitting with Florence, Marco and Fender on the

lawns. I knew the boys were only there for me and Floss, but I appreciated it anyway.

"I heard tell the Kincaids are on the warpath," Marco answered.

Fender nodded. "Same. My old man said there was a bounty out on Vinnie Rossano and Cillian didn't get paid until he had proof of death."

Apollo leant back on his hands. "Yeah. Dad's been pissed. I'm surprised Cillian hasn't pulled in the O'Malleys to be honest."

Marco shrugged. "No one's said anything about a call, but then I've already got my marching orders."

"Valk's built for this shit," Fender said, and I got the feeling it was supposed to be reassuring. "They bred him for it."

"They put him in a fucking coffin for it," Marco huffed, and we all looked at him in surprise.

"A what?" I asked as Marco nodded. "He left that bit out, huh?"

"Is that what Valya was talking about the other night?" Floss asked.

"That or the–" Apollo started, and Marco cut him off with a shake of the head.

"Or the what?" I asked.

I'd known – guessed – that Valen's past was horrific. I'd known that everyone in this circle had varying tonnes of baggage they were carting around from their childhoods. But I never would have imagined that Valen was put in a coffin. I needed to know more. I needed to know he was okay. He was clearly not okay. And I honestly wasn't sure I could handle knowing more.

"It's better you don't know, missus," Marco said quietly. "Not from us. Those are Valk's stories to tell."

"And I'm just going to keep pretending I have no idea what's really going on here?" Fender chuckled, running his hand through his hair.

Marco nodded with a rueful smile. "Aye. You'd best do that, mate."

Apollo took my hand. "The list of people who know about the Morningstar is getting disconcertingly long."

"It's us and Valen."

"Where is Gage?" Apollo asked Marco.

Marco shrugged. "I haven't seen him since last night."

"Does he know?" Florence asked.

"I don't think he's been told but, if this idiot worked it out, then Gage probably has," Marco said, throwing a cheeky wink to Fender, who huffed a rough laugh.

Apollo ran his hand over his chin. "Yeah. All right. He'll keep his mouth shut. But I don't like it."

"I guess we shouldn't be surprised," I said. "Maybe we need to be less conspicuous."

"Valk's absence is certainly helping," Apollo muttered.

I looked down.

I wasn't regretting any of my choices, but I did wish that life didn't have to be so difficult. It was a bed of my own making and I'd lie in it. But it didn't stop me wishing that things could be different.

No amount of wishing, love.

Valen had been right.

Because no matter how much I wished for my life to be different, no matter how often I thought this time it might be, it seemed I was stuck again. But I refused to let them win this time. I would get the life I wanted, no matter how much hardship I had to face in the meantime.

I just had to keep reminding myself that it would all be worth it in the end.

I had to hope that it would all be worth it in the end.

Chapter Eight

Marco dropped me off at the restaurant and I was shown to the back room that Valya had booked for us. Apollo had told me to be there at seven and to look nice. Like I didn't always look nice when we hung out!

But it was almost eight and he still wasn't there. It took quite a bit of convincing on my part to not feel the old sense of trepidation and slight betrayal that he'd stood me up again. That he'd chosen anyone and anything else – probably a Magdalen – over our friendship again. Especially after the strides we'd taken in the past weeks. We were honestly closer than ever now, and yet…

It still stung, but I talked the feeling down until it was less than it used to be.

Then, I called him.

"Where are you?" I asked him.

"Me?"

"Yes, you. I called you. Who else would I be looking for? I thought we were having dinner?"

"Not us. You and Valk."

"What?" I don't know why the idea surprised me.

"Yeah. I got the room for you and Valk. He was supposed to be there when you got there. Is he still not there?"

"Why did you–?"

"You said you wanted to date, spend some time, just exist together. Well, this was the best I could do for now. I had a whole week planned for you both for the holidays, but–"

"Did you tell *him* about dinner tonight?"

"Of course, I did! Where's Marco?"

"Outside."

"Right. Obviously Valk's been held up. Fucking useless surprise that turned out to be. Sorry, Harlow. I'll find out what's keeping him. You and Marco head back to school, yeah?"

I nodded. "Uh, yeah. Sure. And thanks, though. For the thought."

I heard his smile in his words. "Anytime. I want to help anyway I can. You guys are my best friends. I want you to be happy. I want it to work."

"Thanks. I'll go and find Marco."

"Night, Harlow."

"Night, Apollo."

I hung up, gave the servers a pathetic smile and headed out to find Marco. He was sitting at the bar, playing on his phone.

"God texted. Let's head back and I'll deck the fucker later."

I smiled at the sentiment and slid my arm in his as we headed for the car. "I'm sure he didn't mean to miss dinner."

"I'm sure he didn't have to miss it," Marco grumbled.

"We all have higher powers than God we have to obey," I reminded him.

Marco's next grumbled was unintelligible, then he added, "I

don't have to like it. Standin' up the missus, it's unnecessary. Just plain rude is what it is."

On the way back to school, I got a text from Valen.

Valen

I'll meet you in my room.

Harlow

Okay

When I told Marco, he insisted on coming with me. Had I known what his plan was, I might not have let him.

"Where the fuck were you?" Marco asked as soon as he was in the door.

Valen didn't look at all apologetic. He looked pissed. "Busy."

"So busy that you stood up your future missus?"

I though it prudent to close the door behind us.

"In case you hadn't realised, mate," Valen snarled, "we're in the middle of a fucking war. If we can get through it, I'll have the rest of our – hopefully – very long lives to date my wife. Until then, I have to play by the rules."

"I thought you were going to break all the rules for me?" exploded out of me and I wasn't sure why I was so annoyed. I didn't even know who or what I was annoyed at. Just everything, I guessed.

Valen looked at me. "Not if they could get one of us killed, love. Not now this – you and me – is real. I will love you and I will be with you but, when my da says 'jump', I'll ask how fucking high until we get you out of the Callahan contract."

I tried not to believe that the truth of it was actually that he just didn't want to spend time with me. I tried to ignore the fear that he was just another cog in the Nameless who saw their women as possessions to be used for pleasure and breeding, and little else. I told myself it wasn't true that this was all just a game to him – that *I* was just a game to him.

I told myself all that, but the doubt still clawed at me.

"Marco, get the fuck out," Valen barked, his eyes narrowing at whatever he saw on my face.

"If you think we're done here–" Marco started.

"Things are about to get real emotional in here, mate," Valen hissed. "I won't hesitate to show Harlow that side of me, but I will *not* show you."

Marco cleared his throat. "No. Right. Of course. I will leave you to it." He gave me a nod, "Missus," and sidled out.

As soon as the door clicked shut behind him, Valen was in front of me and reaching for me. "Whatever you're thinking, talk to me," he begged.

I swallowed. "It's stupid. It's irrational. It'll be fine."

"I won't have fear festering, love," he said calmly. "There are enough obstacles and poisons between us and our happy ending, let's not add more."

I swallowed hard again. "I'm just scared."

"Of what?"

"Of boring you."

He looked like he was about to laugh. "Why would be scared of boring me?"

I huffed as I ran my tongue over my lip and looked anywhere but him.

It was all very well and good being able to talk to Apollo

and Florence about these things but, if I really wanted to make things work between Valen and I long term, I needed to be able to talk to *him* as well. I needed to put my trust in him, as he had asked, and tell him my fears even if I was worried that he'd think they were stupid.

"I fell in love with you as you are, Valen," I said slowly and he seemed to realise that I was choosing my words carefully to make sure I said what I meant, not that I was avoiding the question. "I don't even know who *you* fell in love with. I don't know me, so how am I expected to think you'll want to be with me when this becomes tame and domesticated? When we're allowed to do more than steal moments and vent our frustrations with sex? What if it turns out that I'm not the person you thought I was?"

A soft smile lit his eyes as he cupped his hand under my ear and made me look at him. "You will always be the person I think you are, love, because I don't expect or want you to be anyone other than who you are in any given moment. I love you for every mood, every passion, every persona you wear and the reason you wear it. I love you because you're strong. You're kind. Patient. You've seen the tip of the iceberg of the horrors of our world, knowing there's plenty worse to come, and you're still determined to make it your bitch. What you choose to do with your life, now you have freedoms, will not change *who* you are or who you are to me."

"What if I take up knitting and strongly encourage you to wear the ugly sweaters that I make for you? The brightly coloured, heart-covered sweaters?" I teased.

The corner of his lips tipped. "Then the Nameless will find

themselves with a few more dead than necessary after they inevitably insult my wife's talent."

It was the second time he'd referred to me as his wife in so many minutes. I knew that was the plan – I *wanted* that to be the plan - but a little thrill of unnecessary excitement still ran through me. As though we hadn't spent so much time talking about the fact that we were trying to negotiate a new marriage contract between my family and his. Like it wasn't inevitable, but just something that we were talking about one day happening in the casually nonchalant way of normal couples.

"Harlow," he said softly as he stepped even closer to me. "I am sorry I missed dinner, love. You have no idea how much I wanted to be there. To pretend that our lives are at all normal and boring, and we can just live them together. Da is…making things difficult."

"How?"

He scrubbed a hand over his face as he stepped away from me. Only one step. "Were I a less cynical man, I'd think he was trying to show me how hard our road ahead is. I'd wonder if he was proving to me why Kincaids don't get to have the job *and* love. That we can't. That the job – the Family – is too much."

"Like he's showing you our future? Me waiting at home for you constantly, you missing important events, me never knowing where you are or what you're doing?" I asked.

He nodded. "Were I a less cynical man. Whatever it *is*, it's a test. I just don't know if he's testing my loyalties – making sure that, if we do this, I'll still be the Family man I've promised I'll be – or if he's waiting for me to be too weak to handle it."

I reached for him and rested my hand on his chest. "Maybe

you should listen to the less cynical man?" I suggested.

He didn't look convinced, but I appreciated that he didn't outright argue with me. Last year, he would have argued with me, derided me, made me feel like the stupidest person in the world for even daring to suggest it. Now, he just looked like he wished he could share my optimism.

"Will you let me make it up to you?" he asked.

Allowing the change in subject, I bit my lip coyly. "How were you planning on doing that?"

"I don't want you to be disappointed, love, but I was thinking we could talk. Maybe watch a movie. Read a damn book next to each other. I don't care, but I want to prove to you that this works as much with our clothes on as when they're off."

"You know as well as I that they don't have to be off..." I sassed.

He wrapped his arm behind me and pulled me to him. "You know what I mean, love."

I nodded, because I knew exactly what he was saying. And I wasn't disappointed at all. I wasn't sure I'd ever get over the way my body reacted to his or the amount I wanted him by just thinking about it, but I also wanted to just be with him. I wanted *him* to want to just be with me. I wanted to make this work long-term and, if that meant not having sex for one night, I was very happy to abstain.

"I do know what you mean," I told him. "What would you like to do?"

He hung his head back for a second, like he was going to regret it as soon as it was out of his mouth. "We have that assignment due. Why don't we…" He seemed to choke a little on the word, or possibly just the sentiment, "study together?"

I pressed my lips together, but a snort of laughter still escaped, and he gave me a look that dared me to laugh again. I took a moment to make sure I could control myself. "Studying sounds great."

"I do study, you know," he said, the most defensive I'd ever heard him.

I blinked, mainly in surprise that he felt the need to say it. "When? I don't think I've ever seen you open a textbook."

"We don't spend every second of the day together, love."

"Aw," I teased. "Are you self-conscious about studying in front of me?"

"I happen to be a lot smarter than I look."

I shrugged. "I don't disbelieve that for a moment."

And I didn't. Even the Saints, who had their lives handed to them on silver platters and had no need for university entrance or marks, needed to keep their grades above a certain level to stay enrolled at Saint Benedicts. For those like the Angels, that threshold was lower, but I knew that every one of them was a lot smarter than I expected their grades suggested.

Still, Valen didn't look like he believed *me*. "I don't," I told him earnestly. "I fully believe that you don't bother putting in any effort, but I'm well aware that doesn't make you dumb."

He looked me over and I watched the expression in his eyes soften. "You are–"

"If you say, 'not like other girls', tonight won't be your only sexless night," I warned him, aiming to be firm but unable to help a smirk.

He gave a rough half-smile in response. "I don't think you are – not to me – but I was actually going to say that you're amazing."

"In what way?"

"You see *me*, Harlow. Not just another assassin for hire for the Nameless, but that I'm an actual person. I didn't even know I wanted to be an actual person."

"I didn't do anything for you that you haven't done for me."

"So how can you possibly think all I want is sex?"

I licked my lip while I worked out how to put my feelings into words. "Because, after a lifetime of being nothing more than the stupid little princess in her ivory tower or on her pedestal, it's taking me a bit of getting used to that someone other than Floss realises I am actually more. We've both been conditioned by this world, love, but we're slowly breaking it. Together."

"I love you, Harlow."

I smiled. "I love you, too, Valen."

Chapter Nine

It was like Cillian was on a personal mission to make sure Valen and I spent as little time as possible together. It was giving me time to collaborate with Dad over the contract specifics, but I'd been procrastinating a bit in the last week since my failed date with Valen and made Florence and Apollo watch a million movies with me.

But, Friday, Apollo was busy.

"What do you think he's doing?" I asked, looking at my phone while I waited for a reply.

"Ten Magdalens," was Florence's sarcastic reply and I chose to leave that firmly where it was.

I was still trying to figure out what they were to each other. I didn't even know if they'd been a one-time thing. If it had happened a few times and was now over, or if they still 'hung out' now and then. She seemed both sardonically amused by usual Apollo antics as well as annoyed by them.

"I'm texting Marco."

It didn't take him long to reply.

Marco

Boy's night. Of sorts.

Harlow

What's that mean?

Marco

Bonfire night.

Harlow

And you didn't want to invite us?

Marco

Not really

Harlow

Why not?

Marco

Because you never seem to enjoy them.

Harlow

I still want to be invited. What if we wanted to come.

I still hadn't heard anything back from him by the time our next movie finished.

"Should we get dressed and see what they're up to?" I asked Florence.

She nodded. "Why not? Maybe Valen made it?"

My heart fluttered. Marco hadn't said Valen was there, but if it was a boy's night of sorts then maybe he was. Then again, if it was a boy's night, then did we want to get in the way of that? Making sure I have plenty of Florence time had been really important the last few weeks. It didn't make up for the time I'd been a bad friend, but it had reminded us both that no matter what bumps or distance were between us, we would always be there for each other. And maybe the boys needed that, too.

Florence rolled her eyes as she pulled off her nightie. "Don't overthink it. If it's a bonfire, heaps of people will be there. We can still go and hang and let them do their male bonding thing."

I nodded. "Good point."

We got dressed – in nothing fancy because it was a bonfire after all – and headed to the clearing in the woods where they were always held. Marco saw us as soon as we stepped into the firelight. He made his way over to us and I saw he wasn't happy.

"What are you doing out here?" he growled.

I looked at him. "Where am I supposed to be?"

"Anywhere that doesn't make my job harder," he hissed, looking around.

I felt my heart shrivel. "You think…?"

He shrugged. "I have no fuckin' clue, missus, and that's the fuckin' problem. They know these woods as well as any of us. Most of the Black Bloods all did their time at Saint Bens. I don't know if they've given up. I don't know how involved Kane is and if he's just waiting for the next opportunity. But I do seriously suspect he rallied a whole fuckin' gang to take you in the first place. So, please, Harlow. Don't be stupid and come to parties in the woods. Go back to your room and stay there. Please."

"Harlow," Florence said earnestly, tugging on my arm.

"Let's just go home."

I did feel stupid. I knew he wasn't calling me stupid, but we both recognised that my actions hadn't been smart. He hadn't replied because he didn't want me there. He – they all – needed a night off and my presence didn't give him that. And I'd told myself that I wasn't going to let my guard down again.

"Harlow!" I heard Apollo's drunken cry.

He staggered over to us, his arms stretched wide.

"We were just leaving," I told him. "Marco made a good point about how it might not really be safe."

"Pfft." Apollo waved his hand dismissively. "You've got four Angels and God to protect you. Come and dance with me. It's been forever since we danced."

I smiled as he took my hand and pulled me closer to the bonfire. "We danced like a month ago."

"That's forever. Dance with me."

I don't know why I looked back to Florence, but I think it was because I was worried that she might read the wrong thing into his actions. If she cared. And she might have. I didn't want to come between whatever they had the potential to have, if there was potential. Her face was neutral, and I felt like maybe I was just reading into things again, so I covered by shrugging apologetically to Marco.

Apollo wrapped his arms around me, and I put mine around his shoulders. His body swayed with mine as the music swelled around us and I let myself just enjoy it. I told myself not to look for Valen; I knew if I didn't find him that I'd be disappointed, and I just wanted a few more minutes of happiness before reality potentially crashed in around me.

"Fuck, I've missed you," Apollo said as he buried his face in my shoulder. I wasn't sure if he was actually talking to me or not. If he knew it was me or not. He was pretty drunk.

"We've spent more time together in the last three weeks than we have in the last three years," I laughed.

He pulled his head up and looked at me. "Do you know how beautiful you are?" he whispered.

"I have been told quite a few times, yes," I answered. "I've tried not to let it go to my head."

He laughed and there was suddenly this look in his eyes. One I hadn't seen for weeks. It was all soft and reverent and warm. It was…

Apollo's lips were on mine as his hand slid to the back of my neck and into my hair. I froze. Something in me heated and jolted and I realised there was a lot in that kiss. And it wasn't just all one-sided. Lingering confusions stirred in me, but they were easy to dismiss; I knew now what my real feelings for Apollo were. Even if he kissed me like… Wow.

I pushed him away as slowly as appropriate for two people who were supposed to be engaged and looked at him in surprise.

"Apollo," I hissed as I heard Marco's exhaled, "Fuck," from behind me.

Followed up with a hushed, "Valk. Valk. Fucking calm down. He's *so* drunk."

I didn't hear Valen's words, but I heard the tone, and he was not happy.

"Get her out of here," Marco said and then Florence was plucking at my arm.

"Harlow, babe. I really think it's time to leave now." She

dipped her head closer to me. "Valen may well kill him."

My heart jolted for a very different reason now and I looked back to Valen. There was definitely murderous intent on his face. I knew how bad it was, because I could also see he was trying to cover it with his usual disinterested boredom, but plenty was still leaking through.

"He's just…" Marco sighed. "He's confused and he's pissed and–"

"That is no excuse," I heard Valen growl as Florence pulled me past him.

I tried to catch his eye, but his attention was firmly fixed on his best friend.

"Babe, leave them to it," Florence whispered to me.

I knew she was right. This was between Apollo and Valen now.

"I will find you later," Marco told me.

I nodded to him, and Florence and I rushed back to our dorm. We got the door closed behind us and I looked at her, aghast.

"I don't know why he did that," I breathed.

Florence sighed as she dropped onto her bed. "I do."

I lost some of the brain fog and went to sit on my bed. "What's that mean?"

She shrugged. She seemed resigned. Like she knew she should have known better. Or maybe I was projecting again. "He's still in love with you."

I scoffed. "Apollo's not in love with me. He's just drunk and fell for our own ruse."

Her smile was sad and there was something in her eyes that made me think I wasn't projecting after all. "Do you…?" I started and her smile both grew and got sadder.

"I don't know. I've been trying not to think about it, honestly. The last couple of weeks, it's become painfully obvious that he really fell in love with you. I know you're out and, even if you weren't, if you both felt the same then I wouldn't stand in the way of your happiness. But...he doesn't have a chance with you. If he and I..." She sighed and I could see she was fighting her emotions. "If anything more serious were to happen between us, how would I ever know if I was just a consolation prize? Can't get the girl, so he settles for the best friend."

"Floss, he'd be stupid not to fall completely head over heels in love with you and realise you've always been the one and what he had with me was nothing in comparison!"

She gave a rough laugh. "And there's the problem. He's not the smartest boy."

My smile was sympathetic. "No. I suppose not. But he's trying to be better."

She nodded. "We are what our world made us."

I shook my head and scooted over to her bed to hold her hand. "Not you. You've always been fiercer, stronger, better than they ever wanted us to be."

"I know. But that's you now. You're becoming better than me. Not just a rebel but a leader capable of real change. I could never be you – the princess you – on any day. How could I ever compare to him?"

I wrapped her in a hug. "Oh, Floss. I didn't know you wanted to."

"I don't know that I want to," she admitted. "But the concern is stopping me from believing that anything could ever be real between us. We have spent a LOT of time together in the last few months. A lot. We've grown closer. I have to admit I don't hate him. It's played on my mind to let it be less casual. He's…hinted we could be less casual. At least, I think he has. But… I just can't get passed the knowledge that I will never be you."

"You shouldn't want to be me," I reminded her. "Come on. Where's my strong, confident Florence who grabs life by the balls and takes what she wants?"

She chuckled and it sounded a little damp. "She's falling into like with a guy who might never stop loving her best friend. I don't… I don't know how to deal with that, babe. I love that you've grown and found yourself and your voice. You're the one grabbing life by the balls now. Life and the fucking men who run it. But seeing him kiss you tonight had shaken me. Shaken what I thought I felt and made me realise that I *could* maybe feel more. We have potential, Harlow."

"But you think he's still hung up on me."

"I know he's still hung up on you."

I shook my head again. "He's not. He told me he's not. He feels the same as me. We're familial. We got confused by the situation and our hormones and all of that." I took her hands in mine. "He's not in love with me, babe."

I could see that Florence didn't believe me, but she didn't argue any more. "If you say so."

"I do. If he loved me, would he be going to all this trouble to help Valen and I with the new contract?"

She looked at me like I should really know the answer to

that question. And, if I was being honest with myself, then I did know the answer to that question and the answer was; yes, he would. Precisely because he loved me.

I still wasn't convinced, but there was also that kiss…

"Come on," Florence said, wiping her eyes and patting my knee. "Let's watch a movie until Marco gives you the all-clear to go and make up with your future hubby."

Chapter Ten

Marco knocked on the door a little while later.

"You're going to want to see him, I'm guessing," he said.

"Which him?"

He shrugged. "Take your pick. I know I said stay in your room, but I'll take you to them if you want."

"Have you actually got reason to be worried? Or is this just an abundance of caution?"

"Both, missus. I'm not falling into the same trap we did last time. I don't think Kane is done with you, ergo I don't think the Black Bloods are done with you. If I were them, I'd be waiting for us to get complacent before attacking again. But I'm also slightly concerned about how Valk's going to take the whole kiss thing."

I nodded. "Fair. Let's go. Floss, I'll see you in the morning?"

She nodded as well, knowing I needed to sort the shit Apollo had wrought.

As we came towards Apollo's room, I heard Valen and Apollo talking. No, not talking. Arguing.

I just saw Valen shove Apollo and quickly pressed myself to the other side of the doorway so they wouldn't see me. "What the fuck was that stunt?"

I caught Marco's eye. He inclined his head and slipped further down the corridor. Far enough that he probably wouldn't hear them, but close enough that he could watch me while I listened.

"It didn't mean anything," Apollo responded.

Didn't it? If I was being honest with myself, I couldn't fully believe that.

"Consider it a sign of how much I love you that I haven't put my fist through your face."

"I got overexcited. Calm down." He still sounded drunk, but better than he had.

"Calm down? You want me to calm down? You're the one who's using words like 'overexcited'."

"Don't you trust our princess?"

"This isn't about trusting *her*. She's her own woman who makes her own choices."

Apollo scoffed. "Anyone would think you're jealous of me, Valk." I knew it was meant to be a joke. Based on Valen's reaction, it wasn't.

"Of course, I'm fucking jealous!" he spat. "You can offer her the fucking world. You have a lifetime of history and love between the two of you that I will never be able to make up for even if she gives me forever."

"And she still chose you. She's in love with you!"

"And how long do you think it will be before this world ruins it? Before our obligations come between us and she realises she chose wrong?"

For all Valen's words, was I not the only one worried about

all that after all? It seemed one of us wasn't being entirely honest. Although, I can't say I blamed him. I just had to hope that he wasn't hiding his own concerns in favour of assuaging mine. I resolved to have a proper conversation with him later.

"It wasn't a choice," Apollo told him. "It was never a choice for her. You were always hers. And even if it was a choice, I fucked it up, Valk. I let her go when she was mine. You didn't."

"I let her go."

"Out of love! Instead of what I did which was just naïve, arrogant stupidity." It was the first time Apollo had actually admitted such a thing out loud.

Valen deflated a little. "Do you regret it?"

"Every fucking day. I always have and always will love her, but I only realised I was *in* love with her the moment I knew I'd lost her."

That was not what he'd told me in the café that day. He'd been in love with me all this time and I'd thought it was strictly platonic? I'd thought the slight sizzle between us had simply been the residue of what we'd thought we had. Us just getting a little confused again about where the lines between platonic love and teenage lust started and ended. But…it hadn't been that way for him. All this time?

Shit, Florence was right.

But Apollo was still talking. "She is yours as you are hers. I know you two belong together, yet I still regret how stupid I was. But every one of those days, it gets a little easier. And maybe Harlow was the wake up call I needed to do right by the woman I'm meant to be with."

"If you love her–" Valen's voice was choked but Apollo cut

him off.

"Don't do that, Valk. Not now. You're past that. Don't give her up because you think she'll be better off or because you think you're obliged to sacrifice your happiness for mine. She has made it abundantly clear that she wants you. You make her happy. And her being happy makes me happy. She's not mine to want or miss or need, and she'd kill us for making choices for her now."

"Nine months ago, those roles were reversed," Valen said softly. "She wasn't mine."

Apollo gave a self-deprecating huff. "Nah. I think she was always yours. Since the day you first locked eyes at my father's estate before school had even started. But the two of you were such loyal bastards you didn't do anything about it until you had no choice."

"You lied to me," Valen said to him, accusation heavy in his tone.

"I did and I'm sorry."

"Why?"

"Because I knew you'd try to give her up for me. If you knew I was in love with her, you'd probably have killed yourself so she had no choice but to eventually fall in love with me as well."

"I'd like to think I'm not that fucking dramatic."

"Maybe. But you are that loyal."

I could picture Valen scrubbing a hand over his face. "Fuck, mate. Why did we have to fall in love with the same girl?"

Apollo gave a rough chuckle. "I don't know. But all that matters is she loves you and I will *not* come between you. I refuse. I want my two best friends to be happy. It's all I've ever wanted. I'll get over her or I won't, but you have your chance at happiness, mate. Don't fucking ruin it."

"I'm trying. But me da is making that very difficult."

"I know," Apollo sighed. "I know. What can I do?"

"I don't fucking know. I don't think Da's against the new contract in theory. But he doesn't realise how important it is. To him, it's just not. He's got other priorities. Meanwhile, I have to watch Archer parade you two around and…"

"It'll be break soon," Apollo said. "I'll have another look through my father's shit and see if I can find anything that will help our cause."

"And if there isn't anything?"

"Then Dad can just think I'm *really* keen to take over the family business. I'll tell him how excited I am to fuck over the Vanguards if that will help."

Valen's scoff was humourless. "If your da was anyone else, that *wouldn't* help."

"Well then, aren't we lucky my father is an arrogant, misogynistic, narcissistic arsehole?"

"Apple don't fall far, mate," came Valen's rough chuckle.

Apollo laughed and I heard a thump. "Oi. You watch it or…"

Knowing the tension was resolved, I nodded to Marco, slipped away to Valen's room and snuck in. It didn't much matter to me if he came in soon or not for another few hours. I grabbed one of his clean t-shirts from his wardrobe and climbed into his big bed that felt so much more like home than any other bed I slept in. I grabbed the book off the bedside table, and his scent enveloped me as I snuggled into the pillows.

"Hello, love," I heard him say as he closed his door behind him sometime later.

I looked up and saw he had a soft smile in his eyes. "Hey," I said, sitting up.

He drank me in, and I wondered how much of his conversation with Apollo was playing on his mind. I'd been too accurate the other day when I'd said that we were both conditioned – we were all conditioned. Valen's conditioning had him considering giving me up because he honestly thought he wasn't enough, that others came first. And, to make things more complicated, if he was worried that our world would push me away from him, then it wouldn't just be obligation but self-preservation making him consider it now.

"I heard you talking to Apollo," I said quickly, before I lost my nerve.

He paused in pulling off his shirt, but only for a moment. "Did you?" he asked casually.

I nodded. "I thought we were being honest with each other?"

He threw his shirt on that big wingback I still hadn't been game enough to try out, before looking at me intently. "You think I've lied to you?"

"I think maybe you've left out just how much this is stressing you out. You've made me talk about my fears. What makes you think you get to keep yours to yourself?"

He nodded as he came over to the bed and sat on the end of it. "Of course, I'm worried, Princess. There are so many unknown factors. All those fears you've shared, I have them, too. But I also believe we can overcome all of them together. It won't be easy, but I'm already willing to go to fucking war for you, love. Why would that not include fighting to make this work no matter what?" As he scrubbed his hand over his stubble, I crawled over to him.

He reached for me and pulled me into his lap before continuing. "I have no role models for relationships, Harlow. I don't know how to do this. It doesn't come naturally to me. But I'm not sure it needs to…" He paused like he was collecting his thoughts. I waited in case interrupting would lose him his train of thought. "When it comes to you, I don't have to think about it. It's not confusing. It just is. It makes sense. I know what I need – want – to do to make it work. There are still unknowns, but knowing I can treat you the way you deserve isn't one of them." He looked into my eyes. "Unless I'm so oblivious I just *think* I'm doing a good job?"

I smiled. "I know 'princess' is a very loaded word for us, but I don't think you could treat me better, Valen. With you, I feel loved and cared for and wanted. But I also feel heard and seen and important. It's not like I have any role models for this in real life either – everything I know about 'healthy' relationships comes from book and movies and TV. And even then, I don't exactly gravitate to the actually healthy ones–"

He nuzzled my face with his. "You got a thing for the bad boys, princess?"

I huffed a laugh. *Jesus, if he saw what I had on my eReader app…* "You know I do, wolf."

His arms wrapped around me tightly as his face pressed into my shoulder. "You have no idea how lucky I am."

I nodded as my hand slipped into his hair. "Oh, I think I do,

Valen. Because that's exactly how lucky I am. You talk – we joke – about me saving you, but you saved me." I fisted his hair and pulled to make him look at me. God, the look of heated desire and love in his eyes when he did. "You didn't even mean to, and you did. You were nothing but you, letting me be nothing but me, and we found each other, love. You don't know how much it means to me. Always meant to me."

"Even when I was fighting you and bossing you around and being an absolute arsehole? he asked.

I nodded with a small laugh. "Even then."

He leant his nose to my cheek and closed his eyes. "Fuck, that day…"

"What day?"

I felt his smile. "The day you refused to obey me and promised me I'd bow before you."

I remembered that day. It was the day I'd just walked in on Apollo and one of his Magdalens, then run into Valen on the way out. It was the first time I'd really talked back to him. The first time I'd been flirty and assertive with anyone other than Florence.

"If I remember rightly, you promised you'd break me that day."

He huffed, a wide smile on his face as he looked at me from under his hair. "You were… Fuck. I knew what you'd walked in on by the state of him. And then there you were, turning me on with your innuendo and your sass and your defiance. Ugh. Your disobedience made me so hard. You took my face in your hand and you fucking purred in my ear. Love, my knee actually buckled, my body was that eager to just bow to you then. But it fucking confused me."

"What did?"

"I saw how confidant and assertive you really were. Then you just…let him fuck around."

"You expected better of me," I said, remembering his words.

"I didn't know why he was so special that you'd just abandon all your morals and strength to just let him get away with it. Even when it stared you in the face. I knew you'd known each other forever, but I'd thought that would have the opposite effect. Instead, you just seemed to fawn all over him like everyone else."

I nodded. "Because I had no say in it."

"You did. If there was one thing I've known since the day I met you both, it's that Apollo would walk through fucking Hell and back for you. All you had to do was put your foot down and he'd–"

I laughed. "No," I clarified. "I mean. I had no right. We… Do you still not know?"

He frowned. "I assume not, then…?"

"Apollo and I were faking it until… God, until he proposed really. I guess." I blinked, wondering when things had really changed with Apollo. We'd never really talked about it until after he put the ring on my finger.

"You what?"

I nodded. "From the day we found out about the contract until…sometime when everything got overly complicated this year, we were faking it. The whole thing. We never *really* dated at all."

"This whole fucking time?" Valen asked, sliding out from

under me and starting to pace. I wondered why he was so agitated.

"Yes. Why? What's the matter?"

"I spent years feeling guilty about the way I felt about you. Years. I spent the better part of *this* whole fucking year beating myself up because I looked at the two of you and– No, I didn't think your relationship was perfect, but you were together and seemed genuinely happy with whatever weird arse arrangement you had. I knew he was in love with you. So, I felt like fucking shit for everything that happened with us because I was betraying my best mate. Then you… You tell me that…" He chuckled, but it was humourless. "I could have had you years ago. And we wasted all that time because–"

"Love…" I said slowly, and didn't continue until he stopped pacing and looked at me. "I… I understand the sentiment. I feel like there's so much more time we could have had together but weren't as well, but the practicality is… If anything happened with us years ago, do you think anything would be different from the start of the year? You and I would still hate each other, and Apollo's ring would be on my finger for real. We needed this, Valen. We needed to wait until now. Now is *our* time."

"That was what he meant after the Wilcox thing? It was all fake?" he asked, obviously needing the reassurance.

I nodded and reached my hands for him. "It was. I thought you knew. At least, I thought you'd found out since. Florence only found out after school started this year. Before that, only Apollo and I knew. I…" I paused, wondering if I should bring it up. I decided to. "I don't know if Apollo really is in love with me, but I realised that I was never in love with him. I love him, of course I do. But he's like a brother to me. He's always been like a brother to me. I convinced myself this year that it was more – that it could be more – because it had to be. I wasn't going to survive otherwise. Especially not after us."

Valen's head cocked to the side as he sat on the bed with me again.

"You said that you'd love me until your dying breath, Valen. I don't know when you knew that, but it hit me pretty quickly. I think I knew after we pretended that we'd fucked each other out of our systems." I trailed my fingers down his cheek. "But I thought we couldn't be together. I thought I had no option but to be happy with Apollo. I didn't *not* want to be with him but, if I'd had any real choice, you know who I would have picked."

"Do I?" he teased.

I nudged his nose with mine. "Yes. You do."

His eyes searched my face, and I couldn't tell what was going through his head.

"Are you okay?" I asked him.

He licked his lip like he wasn't sure. "I'm just reassessing my priorities, love. I gave you up for him once. I thought it was the right thing to do – for both of you. I don't know how much of our…conversation you heard tonight, but the old instincts tried to kick back in again. For a moment of cowardly weakness, I considered giving you up again because I almost talked myself into thinking it was best. Now? Not a fucking chance. You are mine, Harlow Vanguard. You have always been mine. I'm not giving you up again."

"Nice to know you're finally with the program," I teased, and he growled playfully before he kissed me hard.

"Do I need to discipline ye, Miss Vanguard?" he asked, his eyes flashing humour.

I nodded quickly. "I think that would probably be best, Valk. You don't want me getting too *mouthy*, now, do you?"

The corner of his lips quirked as he dropped onto the floor. "I'll give you mouthy, love." He winked at me before he buried his face between my legs.

Chapter Eleven

The Easter holidays saw the first time I hadn't gone to the Callahan Estate during break in I couldn't rightly say how many years. Close to ten, though.

It was the first time I didn't pack my stuff up and drive straight from school to the Estate with Apollo and Valen in closer to five. I was both filled with nervous trepidation and unbelievable excitement that I was going to spend that time with my dad. I wasn't alone though, because, as Dad had asked, Marco came with me. Now that I knew about his contract with Dad and after the incident with the Black Bloods, we didn't have to hide it from anyone else either.

"This is one swanky plane," Marco said as he reclined in the cream leather seat, swirling his Whiskey.

I smiled as I picked up my beer. "It's nothing on the Callahan planes."

He inclined his head. "True. But I've got less cause to be on a Callahan plane, missus. They're not sending a jet for me when I come visiting."

"No. I suppose not. I guess, now this is official, you'll be taking private planes more often."

"Are you suggesting that you'll send the jet for me, missus?" he teased.

I smiled as I looked out the window. "I'm suggesting that, if you're going to stick by me and I'm going to be flying more often, then maybe you'll benefit from the perks of the job."

"I *am* very partial to perks of the job," he said ruefully.

"I'm aware. I'm just not sure how I can get these flights claimed as a business expense," I teased. "What with them being paid for by my father and all."

Marco finished his drink and slid even further in his seat, a satisfied, peaceful grin on his face. "If it's not out of my meagre coffers, missus, I'm not bothered about claiming it."

I laughed. "Good to know, Marco."

"Besides," he said, his eyes closing. "We can have plenty of business dinners."

I couldn't stop the smile that spread on my face. "I'd like that."

His smile was as infectious as it was warm, and I felt a little bubble of that warmth burst in my chest to know that not only did I have Marco on my side, but that I could also call him a friend. I saw the bond that had grown between Apollo and Valen growing between Marco and me. I saw how it wasn't just necessary but inevitable. I relied on him, and he cared for me. I cared for him as well.

As annoying as I expected it would be to have someone literally dogging my footsteps for the rest of my – hopefully, thanks to Marco – very long life, I was also gratified to know that I would never be alone again. No matter what happened. No matter what jobs Valen was called to do, what rifts Archer caused with Apollo once the new contract was in place, how long Florence was in Paris, or what was required of me to help Dad.

Dad was waiting for us by the car when the plane doors opened. Like I was about twelve, I threw myself down the stairs and rushed over to him. He wrapped me up in his arms with a deep laugh.

"It's good to see you too, darling," he said warmly. As he put me down, he nodded over my shoulder. "Marco."

"Kept her safe, Mr Vanguard."

"From all those bottles of the finest Whiskey, no doubt."

Marco winked. "They were looking at her funny."

Dad smiled and inclined his head. "I'm sure. Let's get you both in the car and back home. Your mother is very excited to have you home."

I gave Dad a look. "Please tell me I don't have to intern with her these holidays as well?" I begged.

"No," he laughed. "Why?"

"I have spent years with Frenella going over the household duties, planning parties, being a 'woman'. Don't get me wrong, I love Mum and I like being a woman, but not the kind the Company wants their women to be."

"Then let me put your mind at ease. I have told your mother that I plan to monopolise your time this week. I apologised to her profusely, but she said she understood. I think she's honestly happy for you, darling. A little scared."

"Aren't we all," Marco muttered, and Dad nodded in agreement.

"How much does Mum know?" I asked.

"Everything. I decided it would be best not to hide anything from her. It wasn't in your best interests."

I was surprised by that.

"I know being a woman in a Company Family isn't easy, darling. I know your mother has raised you to survive as one. Given you the tools you needed. I also know that in doing so you didn't always get the support you should have, and we're both sorry for that. We…thought we were doing the right thing and you seemed so happy that we naïvely didn't realise it was necessary. But we love you and we just want you to have everything you want in this life."

"And if everything I want is to destroy the patriarchy and bring the Council to its knees?"

Dad smirked. "Then I would be very happy to do whatever I can to help you." He looked me over as his smile softened and his eyes shone. "I am so proud of you, Harlow. You are by far so much more than I ever could have expected. And I know that's the misogynistic nature of our society showing. I'm sorry I didn't see it sooner."

I leant into him. "We're all a product of our world, Dad. I am painfully aware of this. But we're doing our best to be better. And I think that's all we can ask for right now."

"When did you get so wise?" he chuckled.

"While I was very busy pretending to be the perfect little princess," I replied wryly.

"You will always be my little princess."

Honestly? That meant more to me than I would be willing to admit, even on my death bed.

† † † †

My time at home was amazing. I missed Valen and Apollo and Florence and Fender, but I was spending some quality time with my parents where I didn't have to pretend anything anymore. I didn't have to pretend to be happy about my life. I didn't have to keep quiet about things that would make me seem 'unladylike'. I could actually have proper conversations with them.

"Actually," I said as we were finishing up lunch one afternoon. "I heard that Archer *might*," as in, he did, "have slept with the caterer and Frenella actually fired her."

Mum gasped. "Really?"

I nodded. "And that's why they had to use frozen pre-made food." Which, I personally thought was just as good if not better than the gourmet, specially made stuff anyway. "I heard one of the staff talking about it."

Mum gave a very self-satisfied smirk. "Well, serves him right. I feel sorry for Frenella, of course, for how that would reflect on her. But Archer deserves it, the great git."

Dad smiled as he looked between us.

"What?" Mum asked.

He shrugged. "Can a man not enjoy some family time, Cecelia?"

Mum's eyes narrowed shrewdly. "He can, Reginald. But what was that little smile about?"

"I'm not sure Harlow needs to hear me say it, Sissy."

I choked on my last bite of chicken in surprise at the actual seductive lilt to my dad's voice. I mean, on one hand, fucking good for them. I wanted my parents to be happy and have a good marriage. If me trying to destroy the Company's centuries of patriarchal bullshit did that, then good. On the other hand, I did not need to know about their sex life.

"Rex," Mum chastised as she stood up. "I'm not sure she needed to hear that you're even thinking it."

"And, now she's thinking it," I said, trying not to close my eyes because I knew I'd see it then, too.

Mum and Dad laughed. Mum went around to kiss Dad on her way out and I figured I'd go and see what Marco was up to as well since Dad said he had a couple of things he had to do that I wouldn't quite be ready for yet before my lessons resumed for the afternoon. I didn't ask him if he was getting people killed because I didn't want to know.

"Harlow," Dad said as I made to get up.

I watched Mum leave, then retook my seat. "What's up?"

"How are you?"

Surprised by the question in all honesty. "Uh, what do you mean?"

"You just seem…worried by the lack of progress."

I knew he was referring to the contract stuff, but I wasn't sure what he expected me to say. "I don't know how any of this works, so I don't know what to expect. I guess it's just a little stressful, not knowing what's going to happen or who might get hurt because of my stupid decisions."

Dad looked me over. "Are you regretting them?"

I sighed and sank into my chair. "No. That was… That was unnecessarily dramatic. I'm just…" I sighed again. "I want to be with Valen, more than… Well, more than I should at eighteen. I know it – him, us – that's what I want for my future. I want to marry Valen and take over from you. But," I huffed. "I feel like I'm just waiting again. I've spent my whole life waiting. Waiting for other people to make choices that affect me. Waiting for the day my life finally starts. Or ends. I just kind of hoped that I was done waiting."

Dad nodded. "I understand. I'm sorry it's taking so long. It is frustrating. I'm frustrated, too. Cillian isn't against the negotiations, but he's dragging his heels. He's got other obligations which are taking a lot of his time."

"Vinnie Rossano," I said with a nod of my own.

Dad looked pleasantly surprised. "You know about Vinnie Rossano."

I shrugged. "To a degree. I know he's been causing issues for Archer. I know the Kincaids are meant to be putting him down. As far as I can tell, it's not going well."

"No. It wouldn't be. The Kincaids might be the strongest Brawn in the Company, but the Rossanos are the largest. They've been amassing soldiers for the last decade. While I'm sure Cillian doesn't see them as any real threat, it would be time consuming and annoying."

I nodded as though I really understood any of it. "There is so much history in the Company, and I'm only just scraping the surface."

Dad clearly empathised. "We'll get there. I might have been younger, but I was as ignorant as you are once. One day, you won't remember a time you didn't know the Company inside and out. This afternoon, we'll have another look over the contract draft, and then I want to take you through the books for our warehouse in Spain."

I decided now was the time to have a backbone. "Are you getting people killed first?"

He looked me over and I appreciated that there was full transparency on his face. "Only if they deserve it. What I need to determine is if they do."

I nodded. "What did they do?"

"What they all think they can get away with. We think they've been skimming a little off some shipments."

I took a deep breath. "Can I come with you?"

Dad looked at me, but it was with pleasant surprise. "You want to come?"

I steeled myself. "I have to at some point. Why not now? Why not before I have to deal with Cillian again? Before I have to meet with the Council. Maybe it will help."

Pride emanated from him. I felt a momentary twinge of weirdness that he was proud I wanted to witness a potential execution, but that was what this world asked of me. If I was really determined to be worthy of inheriting Dad's empire, then I was going to be calling shots like people's executions one day.

One day had to come sooner or later, so why put it off?

Dad nodded. "Okay. But I have one stipulation."

"Because everything is a negotiation?"

"Exactly."

"What is it?"

"I want you trained to handle a weapon. Marco's good at his job and he's only going to get better, but there are times you'll need to be the show of force. Most of the people you'll be dealing with will be physically bigger than you. They will underestimate you even after you've proven your worth a million times–"

"Like Archer."

"Like Archer. You'll need to resort to sheer force of will, which is already becoming formidable, but a gun never hurt."

"Valen will have something to say about that," I guessed.

"Valen serves you as much as he loves you. He will see the necessity and, while he may not like it, he will both support the decision and no doubt demand to be the one to train you."

He was right. Of course, he was.

"Tell Marco we leave in half an hour." Dad stood up. "And Harlow?"

"Yes?"

"Just a suggestion, that you are welcome to ignore, but it might benefit the situation if you continued…looking the part."

I understood his meaning. "Keep them guessing?"

He inclined his head. "Keep them guessing. The most terrifying thing to a man in the Company is not knowing exactly what a woman is capable of. Give them the princess and, when it's necessary, show them just how ruthless you can be."

I could do that.

Chapter Twelve

Those guys did get killed. Their biggest regret seemed to be having a woman at their executions, which only made Dad keener to put them down. I walked away with a bit of blood splatter on my dress and my head held high. Because I'd seen the look in the eyes of those still living when they'd seen my reaction, or lack thereof.

I was feeling a little conflicted over the whole complicit in seemingly cold-blooded murder, but I was also feeling really good about my ability to actually take over from my dad, to cement the contract with Cillian, and to face the Council with some hope of winning.

Dad and I were in his study going over some of the business logistics and policies when he stretched somewhat ominously.

"We were talking about the future the other day and I wanted to talk to you about next year," Dad started, and I looked at him in surprise.

"What about next year?"

"Well… I wanted to talk to you about what you wanted to do."

I frowned, still confused. "Do about what?"

He shrugged. "Well, you have no *need* to go to university in order to take over the family business. I can teach you everything you need to know very easily and it's not like most of the Family Heads ever set foot in any educational institution beyond what is legally required, unless it was on a job. But you are more than welcome to enrol, if you like. If there's something you'd like to study."

I blinked as I thought about it.

As a woman in our world, I knew that all previous expectations for me post-high school was to be a socialite with very little brain, but was there something else I *wanted* to do with my life? The option to take over the family business was on the table, and it was honestly all I could think about now. I wanted that. I couldn't see any other future for myself. I would be the Head of the Vanguard Empire and I would make sure that no one screwed our family over again. I would pioneer the way for women in the Nameless, and I would find my way into my father's seat – after his very distant death or retirement – and I would make sure they gave me a voice.

If I didn't need university for that, why would I bother?

Florence had always had her eye on Art School in Paris, and she was very nearly there. She had one more round of retreats to go and she was in. We would be separated at the end of the next Summer regardless of what I chose to do with my life.

I licked my lip and I thought about how to answer Dad; it felt like an outright 'no' wasn't the answer he was looking for. He'd told me when this all started that everything in life was a negotiation. Maybe I needed to negotiate with myself. Think about the answer more before coming to a decision. Who knew?

Maybe, after a little thought, I'd feel like a Business Degree would help.

"I'll definitely think about it. Nothing comes to mind right now, but I'm not going to discount it," I told him.

He nodded once. "Okay. Good. I'm glad."

"Do you want me to go to university?"

"I'd like you to know you have the option and I want to make sure that the constraints our world has thus far placed on you don't ruin the future you can build for yourself. We're breaking all the moulds and all the rules now, darling. We don't have to stop at marriage or inheritance. Why not shoot for the stars?"

I grinned. "Because if we fall short, we'll still end up on the moon?"

He nudged me playfully. "Exactly."

Which was a fantastic sentiment, but only time would tell what the reality held. I knew, if we didn't play it right, that everything could still just crash right back to Earth before it even got out of orbit.

† † † †

The break wasn't taken up just with spending time with my parents and Marco. Thank God. As much as I enjoyed it, I might have gone mad. Not from the lack of the others – per se – but rather the presence of people I wasn't as used to.

So, I was eternally grateful that Valen insisted on calling me at least once a day, even if it was for less than five minutes and we were both half asleep. We took whatever time we could.

That day, the conversation was a little heavier than usual.

And a lot less sexy.

"We've had news from Fender," Valen said.

I frowned. "Fender? What's he found out?"

"We have a fucking traitor in our midst is what." I could feel the fury in him through the phone. I could imagine him pacing like a caged animal. "Gage tried recruiting him to the fucking Black Bloods."

A chill spread over me. "Gage is a Black Blood?"

"Aye. We think that must have been how they knew how to find you and Florence. He was with Marco when you two slipped off campus. Fucking turncoat."

"What are you going to do about it?"

He sighed heavily. "Every fibre of my being demands I put him in a shallow grave–"

"Can I make a suggestion?" I said slowly.

"What? You want to do it?" he chuckled, but there was no humour in it.

I mean, I did. But no. "I'm sure you already thought of it, but why not use him for information? Get Fender to pretend he's thinking about turning and find out what he can about the Black Bloods, how involved Kane is, all of it."

He was silent for long enough that I knew he was thinking. Finally, he said, "I didn't really think of that. No. I was too fucking emotional about it to get that far yet. It's a good idea, love."

"Will Fender be okay with it?"

Valen huffed, and there was slightly more humour in it this time. "For you? Fender'd sign up for the matching jockstrap for you, love."

I laughed. "As long as he's okay with it."

"It's part of the job, love. I'd do it myself, but there's no way I could pull off being disloyal to my God's woman."

"I'm *your* woman," I reminded him gently.

"I know, love. But they don't. And we need to keep it that way until my da gets his fucking act together."

"Dad and I sent him the draft today. He said he'd look over it and get back to us as soon as he could with his notes."

"He'll want Walton to look over it as well. Da's savvy, but he'll want as many eyes and minds as he can trust on it."

"Makes sense," I said. "If we want this to work, it doesn't just need to benefit both sides, but it has to satisfy the Council as well."

"Benefitting both sides will go a long way to satisfying the Council. If it's mutually beneficial, they'll have less claim on Legion. While Legion may be a side effect, the argument can be made that that's not the purpose of the contract."

"Dad said to downplay how emotion-driven this agreement is…" I said slowly.

"Your da's a smart man, love. The Council won't give a fuck how much we love each other. They're business-minded. Love has no place in our world. It's irrelevant. The argument might be useful as a tipping point, but we need the Council already leaning towards deciding with us before it'll make a difference."

I breathed out heavily. "I feel like I'm starting to understand this world without actually knowing anything. So much makes no sense."

"The Company is old, princess. We have laws and codes that

hark from a much older, simpler time. It's not like it was set up last week by equal-opportunists. We're filled with layers of amendments that can quite often contradict something else. The Council's ruling is known to be whim and discretion. We can only lean on the laws and hope they agree with us."

"I miss you," I told him.

"I miss you, too, love. What I wouldn't give to just see your face. Fuck, I'd take seeing Apollo kiss you again just to remember you're real."

"I take it the war's not going well?"

"Define well, love. For every one we lose, they lose five and it still feels like we're no closer to Vinnie. I don't know where they've got all their power. It's like they've got a fucking replicator machine or something."

I heard Neo's voice in the background, followed by Valya's. I didn't hear the words, but they were clearly arguing again.

"Fucking hell," Valen sighed, and I heard a door close. "I might kill them, love. I might actually kill them for just one fucking second of peace."

"Marco thinks they need to fuck and get over it."

He sighed. "As weird as that would be for me – my brother and my sister – that would be preferable."

"Were we that bad, do you think?" I teased.

His chuckle was rough and, after almost a week without him, my whole body came alive at just the memory of what he could do to me. "Oh, we were worse, love. But at least we kept it to ourselves and didn't make everyone else fucking suffer."

"Do you think they will?"

"I try not to think about it."

"I'll go and speculate with Marco, then, shall I?"

"Ye'll have a better conversation," Valen huffed, humour in his voice.

"When are you getting back to school?"

"Monday. Da wants the whole family on Sunday. Fucking Catholics." Like we weren't all Catholics. "When are you planning on getting back?"

"Floss and I agreed to movie night on Sunday since both our families will be done with celebrations, so sometime then. Marco said he's quite happy to just be dragged around at my whim."

Valen's laugh was somewhat bitter. "I'm sure he is. Must be nice to have only one obligation."

"I'm sorry–"

"Don't be. It's the nature of my contract with the Callahans. Da was very careful to make sure I was still beholden to the Family as well. You had nothing to do with it. Unless you count sitting on the stairs and taking my fucking breath away."

I didn't even try schooling my goofy smile because he couldn't see it. "No. But I'm an obligation now, aren't I? That can't be easy."

"You're not an obligation, Harlow." His voice brooked no argument. "You are the thing that makes my sorry life worth living, love. I live for you. You're oxygen and water. You will never be an obligation. You are the only thing I want and fuck the Kincaids and their rules telling me I shouldn't."

"I love you."

I heard the smile return to his voice as he answered, "I love you."

"Valen?" I heard Neo's muffled voice.

Valen answered in Scots, then came back to the phone. "Sorry, love. I've got to go. I'll talk to you later."

I nodded, even knowing he couldn't see me. "Later, then. Say hi to Valya for me."

"I guarantee she returns it. Bye, love."

Then he was gone. I dropped back onto my pillows and missed the way his scent enveloped me in his bed.

"Soon," I reminded myself. "I'll see you soon."

Because I would. One day, we'd have the luxury of time. Until then, I'd take every day that was given to me and be glad of it.

Mum did make it better when I realised just how much she was on my side when I joined her for a pre-bed tea after talking to Valen.

"Oh, I just thought of something," Mum said warmly, and I looked to her. She was smiling widely. "You can get married in Scotland now."

I looked down to hide my grin, so she didn't think I was making fun of her comment. I was just legitimately heart-warmed by her enthusiasm.

"You figure because he's Scottish, the Kincaids will go for the castle?" I replied.

She made a noise of confirmation. "That will put a right bee in Archer's bonnet."

I snorted. "I think me marrying outside his family will be enough."

She laughed and I looked up to find her nodding. "That it will." She sighed happily. "I'll say, darling. The idea of you marrying Apollo was thoroughly romantic. Childhood friends turned sweethearts. It was perfect. But then…" Her smile grew more sincere. "Marrying for true love. Baby, that's more than I had ever hoped for you."

Jesus, that was both horribly depressing and such a lovely sentiment. "We have to avoid all-out war first," I reminded her.

She nodded. "No. I know." She shrugged like she honestly thought that was a formality. "Between your father and the Kincaids? My bet's on them, darling."

I had to have faith that we were going to see this through. But that happy ending seemed so far away right now that I had no idea what it might look like. I was too afraid to picture it too closely in case we never made it.

Chapter Thirteen

We were all finally back together on Monday night and we met in Apollo's room after dinner as though we just needed the comfort of each other's presence. Gage was noticeably absent, as he had been lately. Though at least we knew why now.

"I haven't got much usable out of him," Fender admitted, sounding like he was apologising. "He's cagey. Wary."

"With good reason," Valen huffed. He shifted as though contemplating getting up, but he just tightened his arm around my shoulder. "If he's got any brain left, he'll know the likelihood of two Angels turning is fucking astronomical."

"He obviously thought it was possible enough for him to ask in the first place," Apollo said, his eye on Fender like he wasn't quite sure who to trust anymore.

I shook my head. "Don't do that," I told him. "Maybe that's why he asked? He wants to drive a wedge between us?"

"What good does a fucking wedge do?" Apollo muttered.

"Makes it easier for Kane to get his hands on Harlow," Fender said solemnly and every looked at him. He nodded. "That's the most definitive thing I've found out. Or at least, based on the fucking cartoon hearts that bug out of Gage's head whenever Kane is mentioned, I'm pretty sure our guess is right, and he's taken over the Black Bloods. Gage didn't say in so many words, but I get the feeling that Harlow is endgame."

"Kane's fucking dead," Valen snarled as slipped out from under me and stood up.

"You can't kill him," I said. "Not until the contract is done."

Valen whirled on me, not bothering to leash the full force of his fury. "Why? Why should he get to hover? Threatening you at every turn. We have no idea when he'll make his move. We have no idea how long he's been planning or what he's planning. He has a fucking Angel in his pocket. We have never been more vulnerable.

"You can't think that way," I told him.

"He could come from fucking nowhere and what if I'm not there? What if Da 'needs' me? How am I supposed to face every threat?"

"With us, like always, mate," Marco said earnestly.

Fender nodded in agreement. "Harlow will always have as many of us as possible."

"I want two of us on her at any time. No fucking excuses. Then, as soon as this contract is signed, I'm dealing with Kane."

"That is not the worst of our problems," Apollo said, almost reluctantly.

I was not the only one to say, "What?" in utter disbelief.

Apollo nodded, dragging his hand through his hair. "My dad was the reason Rex needed 'saving' in the first place. He orchestrated the whole thing to get leverage for our contract. I don't know how long he was planning it, but he thought of fucking everything. His contingencies had contingencies."

"That's taking blackmail to a whole new level," Valen said.

Apollo looked at him and I was sure a whole tonne of meaning passed between them. "That has to be grounds for breaking the contract?"

"It's *a* ground," I said carefully. "But what proof do we have Archer was behind it?"

"That's going to be the tricky bit. All I have is the word of a Rossano."

Valen huffed a disbelieving laugh. "Are you fucking kidding?" he asked. "After everything we've been through this year with the fucking Rossanos, we're relying on one of them to help?"

Apollo levelled a steady gaze on him. "For now."

Valen shook his head. "No. No fucking way. We can't trust those fuckers."

"We have to," Apollo said. "The whole reason Vinnie waged war on Dad?"

Valen shrugged. "What?"

"Was because Dad stopped holding up his end of the deal for their part in Dad's scheme."

I could tell Valen still wasn't convinced. That, or he just didn't want to believe it. "This fuckery just keeps getting better and better, eh?" He scraped his hand over his face. "Fuck. Right. We're supposed to meet with Da again about the draft contract this weekend?"

"Saturday evening," I confirmed.

Valen nodded. "Saturday evening. If we can get to a Rossano on Friday night, then we might have some more negotiating power."

"You're going to meet with a Rossano under a peace flag?" Apollo snorted.

Valen glared at him. "I'll do whatever it fucking takes to get my goddamned happy ever after. If that means meeting with fucking Vinnie Rossano or one of his lieutenants, then that's what I'll fucking do."

"Will he take the meeting?" Florence asked.

"Oh, he'll take the meeting," Marco said.

Valen sighed. "He's nothing if not a curious bastard." He looked at Apollo. "And I'm taking a Callahan with me as well."

"That leaves me and Fender with Harlow. You'll need more backup."

"I'll take Neo and Valentina."

Marco laughed at the extreme discomfort on Valen's face. "They fucked yet?"

"What do you think?" Valen snapped.

Apollo stood and shucked his shirt as he headed for the bathroom, and something caught my eye.

"What is that?" exploded out of me and Apollo looked at me with a shit-eating grin.

"You like it?"

I blinked. "When did you get a tattoo?"

Marco huffed a laugh. "When we all got drunk at Fender's mum's place and the Goddess' Angels got matching ones."

The other three boys lifted their sleeves to show me identical tattoos on all their biceps. I got up to look at it more closely and saw it was the Vanguard crest, with a tiara on top, and flanked by two big wings.

"You think you're tough enough to be an Angel?" Florence

121

teased Apollo and I snorted.

"Maybe if he was mediating between the Saintlings," I laughed.

"Ah, he's coming along, missus," Marco said cavalierly, and I noted the return to my previous moniker.

"And just whose missus are you getting ready for me to be now, Marco?" I asked him pointedly. He'd been calling me 'missus' again for months, but it didn't hurt to tease him about it.

He had the decency to look slightly chastened. Then he pointed at Valen. "Valk's, of course."

"Four Angels shall there ever be, to help uphold Goddess' sovereignty," Apollo recited. "Just doesn't have the same ring to it."

"All right," Marco said. "What about 'four Angels shall protection shower, to help uphold goddess' power'?"

"Four Angels will always patrol, to help enforce goddess' control," Apollo suggested.

"Four Angels will e'er companion our fair goddess' dominion," Fender suggested.

"E'er?" Apollo laughed. "That's fancy."

Fender inclined his head towards me. "Fancy word for a fancy lady."

"That's my lady," Valen warned him.

"That's all moot," I said with a laugh of my own. "Not that Valen's lady part. But I'm hardly worthy of having my own Angel squad."

All four of them shuddered.

"Angel squad?" Marco objected.

"That's demeaning," Fender pointed out.

"We're way tougher than that," Apollo added.

"I'm going to allow it," Valen said.

"Aye, because you're literally fucking pussy whipped, mate," Marco laughed.

"And don't you forget it," Valen said to him with a smile.

On Saturday, Fender and Marco were ferrying me to meet with Cillian. As far as we knew, Valen and Apollo's missing the night before had been far more successful than any of us had dared hope and I was hopeful about the outcome of our meeting.

"This whole taking separate cars is a fucking pain," Marco griped as we drove. He was sitting in the back seat with me, behind Fender in the front. Marco had begrudgingly admitted that Fender was much better behind the wheel.

I smiled. "And what happens if one of us is waylaid?"

"Waylaid by what?" Fender scoffed, throwing me a wide smile. "A random sheep on the road?"

I shrugged. "I don't know. But at least it gives the illusion that Valen and I are coming from different sides. Quite aside from the fact we're coming from different places this time."

"I guess. It seems stupid to me, but then less targets in one car is always beneficial."

"The Nicolas boys still causing the Callahans trouble?"

"Who isn't giving the fucking Callahans trouble?" Marco huffed. "You are well shot of that family, missus."

"I still have Apollo."

He nodded. "Aye. Ye do."

One of my favourite songs came on the radio and I turned it up. Marco fake-gagged at me, but it wasn't long before he and Fender were both singing along with me at the top of our lungs.

Naturally, that was the point at which something slammed into the back side of the car on Marco's side.

I think it was on its third full spin when my head hit the window, and everything went black.

Chapter Fourteen

The first thing I noticed was a throbbing headache. My mouth felt thick and heavy and dry. And I was cold. So cold.

"Marco!"

My eyes flew open, and I sat up as the panic hit me.

Marco. Fender.

Where were Marco and Fender?

Something – or someone – had hit the car. Their side of the car. I vaguely remembered blood. Lots of blood.

Fuck. Were they okay?

Because they sure as shit weren't in the dingey little room with me. There was very little in the room with me. Not that I could see anyway. It looked like some abandoned office with most of the furniture removed. There was just a chair and a couch that I wouldn't have chosen to touch with a ten-foot pole. Then again, it looked cleaner than my accommodation; I was on a disgustingly gross mattress, my ankle chained to a hefty bolt in the wall. The shackle, chain and bolt were the newest, cleanest things in the place.

The walls were peeling. There were dubious stains everywhere. The internal windows were broken, and the external ones were boarded up. There was a single, grimy, naked bulb in the ceiling that was giving off the dimmest, dankest light.

"You're awake," came a voice that haunted my nightmares as the door opened.

I turned and my worst fears were confirmed.

"Kane." My voice was strong. It didn't shake, despite the fact my whole body did. And not just from cold.

There was a mad fervour in his eyes as he looked me over and he licked his lip like he was trying to work out which of the obscene things he had planned he should do first.

"Interesting that your first concern is the little guardian angel."

I stiffened. The way he said that, he knew exactly what state Marco and Fender were in, and probably where as well. "Are they here?"

Kane's lips tipped but, unlike the rest of the Kincaids, there was absolutely nothing pleasant or enticing about it. "I left them in the wreckage. Who knows how long it took for them to get there?"

I took a shaky breath, but it didn't stop my heart racing or the lump forming in my throat. "If they're dead–" I started.

"You'll what, princess?" he asked, crouching in front of me and cocking his head to the side. He looked so predatory and detached from anything that could possibly make him still remotely human. "You're at my mercy now. *My* toy. I get to play now."

I swallowed. "Apollo will–"

Kane laughed and it lanced through me. "The little

princeling will wait for Valen to save you, like always. He'll spend his time fucking any idiot who'll spread her legs and tell himself that you'll be fine. But I'll let you in on a little secret, *Miss Vanguard*, you won't be fine this time. Not by the time I'm done with you."

"Then just kill me already, Kane," I dared him. "What are you waiting for?"

He chuckled as he stood up. His hands went to his belt, and I felt my stomach threaten to repeat on me. But he just hooked his thumbs over the buckle and looked down at me.

"I want to know what's so good about the little Vanguard bitch that my little brother would betray not only his God but his Family."

"I don't know what you're talking about," I scoffed, holding my own quite believably.

"What I want to know is why you'd pick *him*. I can understand the desire for a Kincaid man, baby doll, but *Valen*?" He huffed a humourless laugh. "He is the weakest, scrawniest, stupidest one of us. And Kincaids aren't exactly known for our brains."

"Pick Valen?" I said, incredulously. "Why would I have picked Valen? I'm engaged to Apollo, Kane. Valen is nothing to me but his God's tame wolf. He obeys none but Apollo and your father. He certainly couldn't give two fucks about me."

Kane gave me the sort of smile you reserve for someone being adorably stupid. "Aw," he chuckled, and it filled my veins with ice. "We're not *that* stupid, baby." He crouched in front of me again. "You like it when I call you 'baby', don't you, Harlow?" He grabbed my throat and pulled me towards him. "You like it when the men tell you what to do. You all pretend you don't. You put up the fight because you're supposed to. But I know you." He pressed his nose to my cheek, and I did my best to hold what little ground I had. "You want it rough. You want it to hurt. It's okay, baby, I can make it hurt for you."

I mean, it was literally the last thing I wanted. Valen and I had tried that and, if it was him, I did want to give it a go. One day. But out of curiosity and because I had so far loved everything else Valen did to me. Not because the idea of pain itself got me excited.

"I'm going to show you that you chose the wrong Kincaid, Harlow," he continued, his voice low and I was very sure he was aiming for seductive but had completely missed the mark.

Chills ran over me and it was all I could do not to recoil from him for fear it would anger him quicker.

"I didn't choose a Kincaid," I reminded him.

"Come now, Harlow. I know. I *know* about the negotiations!" he yelled, standing up as he tapped his head. More like hit it. Whether in frustration or just insanity, I wasn't going to do anything that might make me find out. "You think you're actually hiding it from anyone? You think Gage didn't come grovelling to me, desperate for approval that he told me everything."

Well, it was nice to know that our suspicions were so easily confirmed. Good old villainous monologues. "And I suppose you're not doing this for anyone's approval. Are you, Kane? There's no jealousy or inadequacy fuelling this little plot, is there?"

He snarled as he took a threatening step towards me. I jumped but held myself firm.

"This had nothing to do with the fact that Daddy loves Valen better," I sneered, all saccharine sarcasm. "That he trusts Valen better. That he believes in Valen more. That *everyone* chooses Valen over you."

"You admit it, then?" he asked, perverse victory in his tone and at his lips.

"You're too smart for us, Kane," I told him, hoping that walking the fine line between insult and flattery would get me everywhere. "What's the point? You know everything."

He nodded. "I do. I do know everything. I know Valen's wanted you for years. And you were no better. So-called God must be even stupider to not have noticed you both fucking right under his nose."

I didn't not like how sure he sounded about that. Like he actually knew how long Valen and I had been together. Like he knew all of it. Just how much did Gage know? And how? Or, even worse, was it not all Gage? Kane had certainly been around enough to maybe have picked up more than he should have. I hid my fear as best I could and tried to work out if there was any way of getting out of this alive.

From what I could tell, the sun was still up, but it was getting late in the day. I should have been meeting Cillian by now, surely. But how much time had passed? How long had they been missing us? Unable to get hold of anyone? How long would it take them between realising something was wrong and finding where the car went off the road?

"Were Marco and Fender alive when you took me?" I asked

him gently.

His head twitched and I knew that whatever shred of sanity he'd been holding onto all these years had finally left him. What was it that pushed him over the edge? It could not have just been that Valen and I were together. That would have been lunacy. Then again, the guy in front of me was the dictionary definition of lunatic just then.

"One of them sure was. His aim was wide. Too wide. I put an extra bullet in him just to be sure he didn't misbehave again."

I gave him a slow nod, ignoring the bile trying to climb out of my throat. I suspected it would be useless to ask him who it was. I wasn't sure that it mattered anyway. If he'd shot them, at least one of them was dead and I didn't think I could handle it being either of them. "Okay. Thank you, Kane."

He twitched again.

Was that the way to get to him? To put this – whatever unpleasant thing he was planning – off a little longer? Play nice. Play sweet. Dad seemed to think that the princess was going to work on the rest of the Company. Maybe it would work on Kane as well. After all, that's what he knew me as. That's what he seemed to respond to. It was the sass that seemed to agitate him more.

"Kane," I said slowly. "I'm not feeling very well. Do you have any water? Or food?"

He looked at me and I was sure there was a touch of concern in his eyes as his eyes roved over my body. "You don't need to be well for what I have in mind, Miss Vanguard."

Okay. I should have guessed. "And what do you have in mind, Kane? What very clever plan have you come up with? I bet you thought of it all by yourself, didn't you?"

Shit, that might have been too patronising. It was like I'd forgotten how to properly tread the line between simpering and passive aggressive. But Kane didn't seem to notice as an eerie smile crept over his face.

"I took you right from under them," he said, clearly very pleased with himself. "I knew it was a matter of time and they'd relax. I couldn't do it at school, but I watched. My Black Bloods watched. We worked at the estates. We kept tabs. We followed. Every day, I was so close to touching you, but I had to wait until my little brother was busy. While Da held his attention."

My blood had chilled to the point I was pretty sure it didn't even flow anymore. He'd been that close to me this whole time, and no one had noticed? How? How had the Black Bloods infiltrated the estates and none of us knew? How dumb were we? Or how deranged was Kane that even Valen hadn't thought it a possibility?

"What do you want, Kane?" I whispered.

"What I've always wanted, Harlow. You. And you're finally mine. I can do whatever I want with you. I can take my time. Neo's not here to save you this time, and the tame wolf sure as shit won't make it here in time."

Make it here in time.

He said it as though even the timing had been planned. As though he had a list of things to accomplish before he thought Valen would be there. Was there a chance that Valen would know where we were? Could I stall Kane for long enough?

He gave me another of those chilling grins. It lit the lower half of his face, but the top half – his eyes in particular – were dead. Like he was just going through the motions. Like he truly didn't feel anything.

Then he pulled his phone out of his pocket, and I watched as the humour did make it to his eyes, if only barely. "Oh, bless. The useless whelp has finally realised you're missing," he laughed under his breath.

It wasn't his phone. It was mine!

If it was mine, then surely the Angels could track…

Kane was watching me with a sordid glee, as though he could see my brain working it out. If he was happy that… It confirmed everything I'd thought.

"You want them to find us."

He nodded. "Eventually. I turned your phone on when you woke up. I'll bet the little runt's had someone scanning for your signal since he realised there was radio silence. The question is whether he's found the car yet?" He put my phone to his ear. "Tick tock, Valen. Can you get here before I'm finished?" He gasped sarcastically, the humour shining brightly in his eyes now and a shudder rippled through me. "Can you save her? She is such a tasty snack, little brother. And I've only had my tongue on her so far."

Oh, gross. Had he actually? Or was he riling Valen?

I felt so dirty. So much more dirty than post-car crash sitting in grimy surroundings could make me.

"Valen!" I yelled.

Kane stepped towards me and smacked me across the face hard enough to make me cry out audibly.

"Touch her again and it will take a fucking week, Kane!" I heard Valen's muffled scream through the speaker.

Kane put the phone on speaker. "What was that brother?" he asked almost sweetly.

"You heard me," Valen growled. "Let her go and I'll consider making it quick."

"Did you hear, baby doll?" Kane said to me, and I licked the blood from my lip. "If I let you go, he'll kill me quick. I think taking my time with you will be well worth whatever punishment Valen thinks he can serve me."

"I'm not going to tell you again, fucker. If you hurt her–"

"Oh, little brother," Kane laughed. "I don't plan to *just* hurt her. How do you feel about hide and seek? Shall we say you get to put one bullet in me for every body part you find?"

"Kane!" Valen screamed, then Kane hung up on him and turned that mad grin on me. The one that actually reached his eyes. He was picturing all the ways he was going to slice me up, I was sure of it.

"Now, baby..." he purred, but it sent venom shivering up my spine. He pulled a knife from the back of his jeans. "Where do you want me to start?"

Chapter Fifteen

By the time the sun's rays were starting to filter around the boards on the windows, I'd lost count of the number of times Kane's blade had been drawn through my skin. The times he'd left me on the precipice of passing out, only to start again when I returned to full consciousness.

My arms. My legs. My stomach.

Everything hurt. Everything bled. And I had a feeling that he was only just getting started. All night, I'd clung to the knowledge that Valen was coming. I didn't know how long he'd be, but I was pretty sure that Kane's plan was to make sure Valen arrived just in time to say goodbye but too late to save me.

Kane was just dragging his blade over my thigh, carving a little heart shape into my skin, when there was a great clattering and banging coming from somewhere else in the building.

"KANE!" I heard someone roar.

Kane's eyes widened cheekily. "Uh oh, the cavalry's early, baby doll." Then he pouted. "Our time to play has been cut short. But don't worry. There's always next time."

He walked to the door and peered out of the room. I heard

the familiar shouts of Valen and Neo. Kane grinned at me, blew me a kiss, then he was running in the opposite direction.

Valen skidded outside the door and saw me lying on the mattress, covered in blood. I saw the fury on his face. The pain. All the emotion and anger he was going to use to rain down vengeance on Kane when he found him.

"Check her!" Valen yelled back to Neo.

"Valk–" I heard Neo start as he came into view.

"HE IS MINE! Check her. She dies, and you're next!" Then Valen was running off through the building.

I gave Neo a wan smile through the blood caked on my face. "Hey."

"Fucking hell, Harlow," he breathed as he rushed in and dropped in front of me. "I don't even know where to start. What hurts worst?"

I huffed a spluttered laugh. "Everything?" I suggested.

He nodded. "Yeah, that doesn't surprise me." His hands were gentle, methodical and practical as they searched over my body for every single wound. "Fuck, you've got strength, lass. I… I don't have enough shit to fix this in the car."

I shook my head. "It's mostly superficial, I think. He didn't want me passing out too soon, let alone bleeding out."

"And the crash? How much damage?"

"Very little. I hit my head. I think I was lucky."

Neo started looking over my chain. "Luck had very little to do with it, I'm sure."

He yanked on it, and I winced where it rubbed my leg. Then he stood and I pulling something out of his pocket.

"I haven't picked a lock in fucking years," he muttered as he took something out of a little box. "Let's see how this goes."

He got me out in just a couple of minutes. He worked in silence, and we listened to the fighting between Valen and Kane. There was a lot of yelling. Some gunshots. I tried not to focus too closely and pretended it was just background noise. Once my leg was free, Neo helped me hobble out of the room.

Outside was a bigger room, like a warehouse. The ceiling was low, and I guessed the exit was through one of those doors. Valen had Kane on his knees at his feet with his gun trained on his head. Kane was covered in more blood than I was. Valen was bleeding – which made my heart lurch – but way less. There was a knife in Kane's leg and another in the side of his gut. His arm hung limply like it was broken and one of his legs lay under him at a funny angle as well.

"Valk," Neo said carefully.

"Ye want to take him back to Da, don't ye?" Valen snarled, but his eyes were on me, and I saw his whole body was shaking. "Is she all right?"

"Ask her yerself," Neo said.

I knew what this was. Valen had to separate us to do what needed doing. One job, then the other, or he risked just exploding. He had to compartmentalise. If he felt too much for me now, then he wouldn't be strong enough to do what needed doing.

"She's fine," Kane said, and his voice gurgled horribly. Blood bubbled out of his mouth as he smiled at me. "Aren't you, baby doll?"

Valen smacked him in the head with the butt of his gun. "You don't talk to her," he growled.

Kane burbled a bloody laugh. "We don't need words, do we, Harlow. We say it much better…physically."

Valen retrained his gun at Kane's head.

"Valk!" Neo cried, almost letting go of me to step towards his brothers. "Think about this."

Valen's arm shook. "I don't need to think, Neo. I've thought about it. I've spent years thinking about it. Years when she wasn't even mine, dreading a world without her in it. Knowing exactly what I'd do to anyone who touched her without her permission, to anyone who hurt her." Valen looked at Neo, a beseeching calm in his grey eyes. "I will not lose her again."

Valen didn't even blink as he squeezed the trigger. He didn't even look down. His eyes stayed on Neo like the point had to be made. I looked away, though. I looked away and my eyes shut at the crack that reverberated around the room. Neo's arm tightened around me as though it was instinctual protection.

Finally, Valen looked down at Kane's body, and emptied the clip into his chest and head. One shot right after the other, each one within a centimetre of the previous one. He didn't blink once. When he was done, he breathed heavily, his gun still trained on Kane like he was afraid his brother could rise from the dead.

"Where's Marco? Fender?" was the first thing out of my mouth once I was sure Kane wasn't coming back. I didn't know if it would jolt Valen out of the red rage he was drowning in, or if I also just had to know.

Valen's expression didn't change. "Hospital. They… They'll be in there a while."

"Their side of the car took most of the hit," Neo explained.

"They're…still unconscious."

My heart might have stopped for a second. "I need to see them."

Valen put his gun in its holster and stepped towards me. "You need to sleep," he snarled, and I knew better than to take offence at his tone; he was as stressed about the whole situation as me, and he was handling it no better.

"I need to see them!" I screamed. "I *will* see them, Valen. You will not keep me from them!" Marco. Fender. I couldn't… It was all my fault.

"The doctors put them both in an induced coma." Neo's voice was the only one even attempting reason. "Rest first. You won't miss anything. You know it's what they'd want. It's what Marco would want, Harlow."

But I didn't want a voice of reason. "And I suppose you know all about what he'd want for me?" I snapped.

There was a ripple in Neo's pure calm. A twitch in his lip, at his eye. A flicker of emotion. "I won't do you the disservice of underestimating you, Miss Vanguard, but there are still many things in the world that you know nothing of, and you would do well to remember they will never be yours to know. If you refuse to do what is best for you, and Marco loses you because of that, he will never forgive himself." He shook his head. "Never. He would rather be dead right along with you."

He did that thing he and his brother were so good at; saying so much more than their words. My heart caught in my throat as I realised what he was really saying.

"Who did you lose, Neo?" I asked, my voice so tiny now.

He swallowed. "That is one of the things that will never be

yours to know, Harlow." There was no malice in his tone, no aggression. He was simply stating a fact. Something that he might even wish wasn't true, but the need to safeguard his heart was more important than showing me he trusted me, and I could appreciate that.

I gave him a nod to show I understood. "Of course. I'm sorry."

"Don't be sorry. Be smart," was his clipped reply. "Let's get you safe."

"But, with Kane dead–" I started.

Valen nodded once. "The Black Bloods will think again, but there's still clean up."

Neo looked at me. "I would suggest you add that to your list of demands for the contract between our families."

I blinked. "What? Your brother is dead and you're thinking about the *contract* right now?"

"Are you not?" he huffed. "You have serious leverage over our da now, lass. Do not waste it. Kane's actions are no guarantee he'll agree, but they'll go a long way to tipping the choice in your favour. By all rights and laws of the Company, Da owes you reparations. Make sure he gives you revenge on the Black Bloods as well as Valen's hand."

"My hand," Valen scoffed, losing some of his tension. "Am I the one being given away here?"

"Well, it's not your fiancée," Neo said, and the look he gave his little brother was one of such sincere love and sibling teasing that I had to bite my lip to stop myself laughing out loud.

Valen just shook his head and pulled out his phone. "Fine. But let it be known that *I* have chosen this. I knew from the start that I'd be the consort. I am okay with it. I just don't need it rubbed in my fucking face. I'm working on the fragile male ego thing, but I'm not quite there yet." Then his phone was to his ear, and he walked away.

Neo was smiling after him fondly. "Only one other Kincaid in my life has loved as deeply as he loves you, Harlow. We're a bitter, emotionally stunted lot, but he's doing his best."

I smiled as well, deciding not to clarify if he meant himself and the mystery person I suspected he lost. "I think he does quite well, actually."

Neo looked at me in surprise. "Really? Are your standards that low or is he different behind closed doors?"

I huffed a laugh. "He's different, but my standards are probably pretty low as well."

Neo gave me a nod. "Fair enough."

"Do you hate me?" I asked him.

His surprise doubled. "What? Why would I hate you?"

"Because I'm not making things easy for your family. I'm…making a lot of demands."

He shrugged. "That's our world, Harlow. Contracts. Negotiations. Demands. I have no doubt that the Kincaids will be very well compensated for whatever contractual obligations Da signs. And I will be more than willing to confirm them when I take his place should that be necessary."

"Why would you help me?"

"Because Valen is my little brother, Harlow." He paused as though he wasn't sure if he wanted to say what was on the tip of his tongue. Then he ploughed on quickly. "And I want him to have what I never can." Then he cleared his throat and indicated I follow him out.

"What about…?" I looked back to the room where Kane's body lay.

"Valen's organising clean up now. Our job is extraction. Grunts will be in soon to deal with the body and the evidence."

I nodded as I followed him. "Grunts," I said, mainly to keep my mouth from asking him to tell me more about the life he could never have. "It's Brains and Brawn and Grunts."

"It is," he answered, like he too knew that we needed something to stop other conversation.

"And Brains and Brawn both have representation on the Council."

"Aye."

"What about Grunts?"

"Far as I know, there has never been a Grunt on the Council."

"Why not?"

He shrugged. "I guess they have no power. Occasionally, Grunts have worked their way up and then got a spot on the Council. Talk is that Walton is a contender for a position at the next elections."

That surprised me. "Florence's dad?"

Neo looked back at me with a shrug. "I guess."

"How many families can be nominated then?"

He huffed. "I don't know the full numbers. As far back as Da's time, there've only been about twenty or so families who've been elected. Probably less."

"And thirteen serve at a time."

"You're very interested in our politics, Harlow. You

thinking of running?" he teased as we exited the building to what was obviously an industrial area. I couldn't tell, by looking at it, which town we were in.

I smiled. "One day. But I'm kind of hoping to keep my dad alive and healthy enough to keep serving for a while longer."

"I can understand that."

"Understand what?" Valen snapped as he put his phone away. "Leonte's crew will be here in a couple of hours." He looked around the vicinity. "If his body's found in that time, who gives a fuck?"

"Da's gonna give a hefty number of fucks either way."

Valen looked to me. Whatever he was thinking, he liked it. "That's what I'm hoping."

Neo shook his head as he opened the back door of the car for me. "It's a dangerous game, Valk. Watch you don't find yourself in a body bag before you get Harlow down the aisle, yeah?"

"It's not my game, brother," was Valen's answer as I paused getting in the car. "It's my woman's, and she's going to fucking to win it."

Neo seemed to share his optimism but be more hesitant to show it so viscerally. "Let's get back to Da and sort this newest shit out. Between your intel from Rossano and this, I wouldn't be surprised if Da just signs on the spot, but there's no guarantee."

"I will back Harlow every time."

Neo clipped him across the back of the head, but it was a fond motion. "Aye, and yer meant to, ye bampot. For a boy broken to fail at relationships, ye sure do it surprisingly naturally."

Valen looked me square in the eyes and I saw all his love burning there. "I am hers. I've always been hers."

I smiled at him. "And I am his."

Neo fake gagged. "Fucking hell. You two are… I think I'm gonna be sick."

Then he caught Valen's eye and grinned. Actual, pure, positive emotion. Valen tried to fight a return smile, I saw it. But he failed spectacularly. They had a companionable scuffle as we all piled into the car.

There was a blanket in the back, and I said 'fuck it' to seatbelt laws and snuggled up under it to get some sleep.

Chapter Sixteen

I registered the car coming to a stop and pushed myself up. "Where are we?"

Valen and Neo exchanged a glance in the front seats.

"We've made a pit stop," Valen said.

"Apollo called while you were asleep," Neo added.

"Okay…?" I said slowly.

Valen cocked his gun. "We're going to kill a fucking traitor." Then he swung out of the car.

I looked to Neo.

"Harlow–" he started warning me, but I was following Valen as fast as the tiny little cuts pulling on my skin would allow.

They stung more than anything. They were hot. There was a bit of aching. But mainly just stinging when I moved them. I hoped that meant they'd heal quickly and not scar too badly. We were at another warehouse, but I recognised this one as being the one they ran their underground fights in.

The door was open, so I helped myself. I wasn't surprised when I saw that the only people in there were Apollo and Gage. Gage was tied up, semi-crucifixion-style against the fight cage chain. His head was hanging, and I couldn't quite see whether he was conscious or not.

Valen's gun was trained on Gage, but Apollo stepped up beside him.

"Let me," Apollo said.

"You sure?" Valen asked.

Apollo nodded. I had never seen him so cold and calculating. Talk about the school of Kincaid. Whatever training Apollo was undertaking these last few months, he'd either learnt a lot or hidden even more from me beforehand than I realised. "I'm sure. Can hardly claim Angel status if I don't win the challenge."

Valen handed him the gun and Apollo aimed.

"Last words, traitor?" Apollo said.

It was then Gage looked up. He kept his mouth shut. I couldn't decide if it was his last act of defiance or if he knew it was just a waste; he'd betrayed one of the most sacred covenants their group held. To my knowledge no Angel had ever rebelled against his God, and Apollo now had two of them. Even if he condoned Valen's rebellion, Gage's would not stand. I wondered how much of Apollo's desire to be my Angel was borne of him feeling as though he failed the position of God of Saint Benedicts. I hated that he probably thought that about himself, but now was not the time to prop up his ego.

"Then I not only challenge your position but, as your God, I hereby relinquish you of your obligations as Angel. Enjoy the rest of your life."

Gage didn't look away as Apollo fired. The bullet hit him square in the centre of the forehead. I watched the light leave his eyes, feeling oddly desensitised to the violence for one day. I blamed the exhaustion that was still sweeping my body. My head was like cotton wool. But among the wooliness, electricity sparked, shooting adrenalin through me. I felt like I needed to sleep for a week but also like I'd never sleep again.

"As our Goddess' right hand, I hereby welcome you to the ranks of Angel, Apollo Callahan." Valen's words were clipped. Icy. He was an emotionless husk, and I was suddenly the most scared I'd been in the last twenty-four hours about what he was about to do.

"Valen?" I said, stepping forward.

Valen shook his head, turning to walk away.

I took a step towards his retreating back. "Don't you walk away from this now, Valen Kincaid!" I yelled at him.

I saw the smallest falter in his steps, but he kept walking.

"Oh, you are not…" I muttered as I stalked over to Apollo.

"Just give him time–" Apollo started as Neo tried a simple, "Harlow–"

I wrenched the gun from Apollo's hand as I shook my own head. "No. He doesn't get to waste anymore of our time."

Lining up, I loosed a shot to Valen's right. It whizzed past him – not bad for less than two weeks of lessons – and he actually flinched before turning the full fury of all the families Kincaid and Volkov on us. "What in the FUCK?" he cried.

I still had the gun trained towards him and his eyes narrowed when he saw who'd fired it. But it did the job. No longer was he walking away from me but towards me.

"You could have killed me!" he snarled.

I nodded. "Yeah. I guess I could have."

"What the fuck were you thinking?" he asked as he took the gun from me, emptied the clip, and threw it away.

"It seems nothing short of a fucking assault will get your attention and, if that's what it takes to stop you walking away from us, then, love, I'll assault you all you like."

I saw the heat in the depth of those grey eyes, but his expression was otherwise hard and cold. "You'll be better off without me."

"You said you'd never give me up again. You said you wouldn't lose me again!"

"The only way I don't lose you is to give you up. Don't you get that?"

I pushed against him. "You don't get to make that choice. No one gets to make that choice but me! Kane..." My voice wavered and I ploughed on. "He had designs on me since long before there was anything between you and I to speak of. The difference, Valen, is that you had a vested interest in saving me from him now."

"Princess," he sighed. "I would always have had a vested interest in saving you. Even if nothing changed, I'd have come for you, and I wouldn't have hesitated to kill him."

Behind us, I vaguely noticed Neo drag Apollo out to give us some privacy.

"I am safer with you, love. Marco's..." My voice faltered again. For a different kind of grief this time. "He's good at his job, but even he's not as good as having Valen Kincaid by my side, in my bed."

"I'm a liability, love."

"So am I!" I snapped. "I'm Harlow-fucking-Vanguard, in

case you hadn't noticed. The daughter of Reginald Vanguard, one of the most powerful members on the Council of the Nameless. They came for me when I was Apollo's. They came for me now I'm yours. And they'd come for me without either of you in my life. Are you going to leave me with just Marco for protection? Because he's going to do a piss poor job for the next few months."

I could see him wavering, but he was doing what he thought was best for me and I hadn't fully convinced him otherwise.

"After everything we've been through to get here, Valen, you don't just get to walk away. You don't just get to throw it – throw me – away. I knew what I was getting into from the moment I first told you that you'd bow to me. Maybe I was a bit naïve when it came to Apollo, but I have *always* known who you are!" I shoved him again. "Always.

"I love you and I am done having *men* dictate my life for me! So, if you still love me, then you don't get to walk away to 'protect' me. I decide how I need to be protected, Valen, and I will not hesitate to ask. I'm not afraid to be with you. I'm not afraid of who or what will come for me if we're together. I'm afraid of what I'll have to face – alone – if we're not…" My tirade ran out of steam, and he was staring at me in absolute shock.

He had no words. I had no more words. He stepped up to me, cradling my face gently in his hands as he searched my eyes. My hands went to his shirt, and I closed my fingers around the material like that had any hope of keeping him near me. He dropped his forehead to mine and we both breathed heavily.

"Thank you," he whispered.

"For what?"

"For not letting me walk. For reminding me when I was too stupid to remember. When I was too scared to remember." His face nuzzled mine softly. "I love you and I don't want to live without you."

"Then stop trying to walk away, Valen…" I begged him.

He huffed a humourless laugh. "You're not the only one having trouble believing they're worthy, love. You're not the only one who forgets sometimes that this is real. That among the shitstorm of our lives, we found something else worth living for. Something more than revenge or obligation or blood." His hand slipped into my hair and his lips brushed over mine. "You saved me, Harlow, and I'm trying to remember that."

"It will all be easier once we have the contract."

"We'll meet with Da tomorrow. He and Rex are still at the hotel. We'll get a room there, rest, clean up, then you'll storm in there with all your incredible force and power, and you'll bring one more Kincaid man to his fucking knees before you."

Our lips met more urgently. "Tomorrow."

"Tomorrow. Tomorrow, you'll be their Goddess, love. Tonight…" he breathed as he kissed me. "Just let me have tonight."

After one more long hug, we met Apollo and Neo at the car, and we drove to the hotel I borrowed Apollo's phone to let Florence know that I was fine, but I'd lost my phone, and I would call her as soon as rest and negotiations allowed. She didn't like it any more than I did, but she accepted it.

Valen spent the time back on the phone to his father and mine, no one much caring what time it was as long as there was an update that I was safe. We agreed to meet in my father's room at two in the afternoon and there would be copious amounts of food and drink, as well as a change of clothes, to get us through what we all expected to be a long final negotiation.

The four of us checked in. I suspected that we looked a right sight. But the staff who manned the front desk in the dead hours of the morning barely batted an eyelid at the state of us. In a somewhat pointed silence, we all headed for our rooms; Apollo and Neo to theirs, Valen and I to ours.

It wasn't until the door was closed behind us that we both seemed to finally breathe. That we, at the same time, seemed to believe that we were safe. At least for now.

We reached for each other and just stood there in the darkened room, holding each other, for long enough that I was almost convinced I wasn't about to lose him again. A sentiment he was feeling as well.

"I thought I'd lost you for good this time," he said heavily.

"Me, too."

"Oh, love. Let me look at you." He pulled away. "How do you feel?"

"Like I'm not sure I'll ever be clean again."

There was terrible pain in his eyes as he searched mine. "How...? How bad was it?"

I knew what he was asking. I lay my hand on his chest. "Just a knife. He made a lot of promises about what was coming next, but..." I shook my head. "It was just the knife."

He sighed heavily. "I shouldn't have–"

"We can't think that way, Valen." My hand went to his

cheek. "We'll go mad that way."

"What do you suggest we do then, love?"

I ran my face over his. "I need you, Valen. I need you to remind me we're still here. Together. I need–"

Valen kissed me hard, and our arms went around each other. Heedless of the blood. Well, mostly.

"Shower?" I suggested and I felt him smile against my lips.

"Shower," he agreed.

We stumbled into the bathroom. My hands were all over him. His were being very careful about what they touched. I appreciated him being careful with me but...

"If he didn't break me, you won't," I told him pointedly.

"I don't want to hurt you."

"And I don't want you to treat me with kid gloves, Valen. Touch me like you mean it, or don't touch me at all. Understood?"

He grinned at me through his hair. "Understood. You tell me if I go too far, understood?"

I nodded. "Understood."

"Good."

Valen stripped me quickly before he picked me up and pressed me into the wall of the shower. While he kissed me, he turned on the water. It was freezing to start with, and we both cried out in surprise before laughing. It didn't keep us from each other for long, though. Between us, we got the water to a more comfortable temperature, got my underwear off, Valen naked, and all before the blood and grime had finished swirling down the drain.

There was very little gentle about the way we came together.

Valen's hands rubbed over the cuts on my body. Each drop of water or brush against them made them sting, but it reminded me I was alive, that I was with him, that I'd survived and Kane was dead.

Valen spun me around and pushed me against the wall before slamming into me. His hand went to my throat and held me firmly. I wrapped my hand around his wrist and we both used it for leverage. His teeth dragged over my shoulder, igniting every sense in my body. The pain from my wounds was sharp, but I didn't hate it. I actually kind of liked it. Maybe not always, but definitely in that moment.

The moment where we both just needed to know that we were still real. That neither of us had been lost. Not when two of us almost were. Not when so much uncertainty surrounded us. We were simple need and desire and emotion. Our bodies saying everything we didn't have words for. Feelings too strong and difficult and raw to even know where to begin to find the words.

So our bodies did the talking until we finally fell asleep together in the huge soft bed, wrapped in each other's arms; just another language conveying what was so devastatingly important to tell each other in that moment.

Chapter Seventeen

I woke in Valen's arms. Clean, safe and much less sore than when they'd dragged me out of the warehouse.

The bed, on the other hand, was much less clean. My various cuts had streaked blood all over the previously pristine white bed sheets.

"Don't worry, love. They'll get plenty of compensation."

"I suppose you've bled worse on hotel sheets?" I sassed and he grinned at me. I nodded. "Of course, you have."

"Just to be sure, though…" he said slowly as he started kissing over my shoulder and down between my breasts.

"What are you doing?" I asked with a smile.

"Making sure you've clotted. Would be a shame if you needed another shower."

I nodded. "Oh, yeah. Total shame."

He chuckled. I felt the vibration against my stomach, and it made me sigh in pleasure.

Valen did a very thorough job of checking my wounds. He pressed a kiss to every single one of them, taking him a not inconsiderable amount of time. He gently traced the lines of every icon his brother had carved into my skin. Hearts and stars, a couple of flowers, a smiley face. Mostly where I could hide them; the fleshiest, most sensitive, intimate areas like my upper legs, my stomach, chest. Were I not wondering about how permanent each of those marks would be, I'd be impressed with Kane's skill with a blade. The rest of my body was far less artistically decorated, but with no less finesse whether it had been with the blade or Kane's fists.

But, when Valen was done, his head stayed very firmly between my legs. He didn't emerge until he had me moaning his name for the second time. As he did, he looked up at me with a cheeky half-smirk and swiped his hand over his mouth.

"Come here," I told him, coaxing him up my body.

"You not had enough, love?" he teased as he crawled up over me and nestled his hips in line with mine.

I rocked into him, and his tip teased my entrance. "I will never have enough, love."

As he slid into me gently, he kissed me hard. It was slower, softer, saying much the same but in a very different way to the night before. This wasn't raw, unfiltered, desperate emotion anymore. It was what came after the adrenalin wore off. What could be felt after some processing.

Valen's hands traced over my skin as his lips brushed over my cheek, my jaw, my lips. His thrusts were languid and deep, making my toes curl and my hands grip him tightly. The second wave broke over me while I was still basking in the first, and he wasn't that far behind me. And even then, he seemed loathe to let me out of his arms, instead holding me close as our fingers explored each other with no real purpose in mind.

As we were just lying there together, there was a knock on

the door. Valen wrapped a sheet around him, picked up his gun and went to the door.

"Rex," he said.

"I take it she's recovering well, then. Have I come at a bad time?" I heard Dad's somewhat humoured voice.

"Maybe if you'd been any earlier," was Valen's mutter as he stepped back and let Dad in.

"I'm glad she's feeling all right."

I blinked at them as I pulled the remaining sheet up to my chin. "Do you two mind?"

They both looked at me like they honestly hadn't thought about the fact that I might have cared that I was naked here.

"I've brought some clothes," Dad said, as though that was an answer or made any better. He lay the garment bags and shoe boxes on the couch.

I nodded. "Okay. Thanks." I looked at him pointedly, but he just turned to Valen, totally relaxed and at home like the two of them were going to strike up a conversation about the damned weather or something. "Excuse you!" I huffed and they looked at me again. "I love you both, Lord knows I do. But that does not extend to me wanting to be naked while you're both in the room."

Dad smirked and nodded to me. "Of course. What was I thinking?"

I shrugged wildly. "I don't know. Either that I'm still like seven and, in which case, I should *not* have a naked man in my room, or that I'm actually just one of the boys, which is both awesome *and* disturbing. Boundaries, man!"

Dad held his hands up in defence, throwing Valen a

companionable grin. "Of course, darling. Boundaries. I will see you both soon."

I gave him a terse smile and Valen saw him out. When he came back, he looked like he was trying not to laugh.

"What?" I asked him.

He shook his head. "Nothing. I just… Your awkwardness is amusing."

"Amusing?" I huffed. "He knew exactly what we'd been up to in here."

"So?"

"What do you mean, 'so'? In what way is that 'so'?"

Valen shrugged. "So? Are you under the impression he thinks we don't have sex? We're eighteen, love, and talking about marriage. He knows we're having sex."

I spluttered. "That's not… I mean… That is not the same as you two having a conversation while I'm stuck naked under the covers."

Speaking of covers, Valen took a handful of them and yanked them off me. "Those covers, love?"

I tried frowning at him, and it turned more into a smile. "Yes, those covers."

He dropped the ones around his waist and crawled over the bed towards me. With each word he got closer until he was punctuating every few with a kiss to my neck, my cheek, my nose. "You endure torture, watch me kill my own brother, watch Apollo kill what is essentially his brother, *and* try shooting me in the back, and yet you're a little uncomfortable about your da knowing you're naked under some sheets?"

I shrugged. "Well, when you put it like that…"

He laughed and the humour made his eyes shine like silver. "When I put it like that," he agreed before he kissed my lips playfully. "Regrettably, we should get dressed."

I groaned and flopped back on the pillows. "I don't want to. I'm not ready."

He took my hand and pulled me back up. "You are more than ready, love. You know you are. You're a fucking survivor. Now you go in there, march up to my father, and you demand my hand in marriage."

I laughed and he threw me a smile as he climbed back off the bed and picked up the garment bags. "You want me on my knees in front of you while I'm at it, love?" I teased.

He winked at me as he started getting dressed. "I wouldn't say no to later, love."

Resigned to what I had to do to fight for my man, I got up and got dressed as well.

Dad had done well. There was a dark grey suit for Valen with a black shirt, and a white sleeveless but collared, V-neck dress that fell below my knees for me. He'd even remembered underwear and shoes. All in the perfect sizes, of course, because we had people for that kind of thing.

"How very virgin princess," I muttered as I pulled it on.

As he turned to me, Valen was raking his hand through his hair. He paused halfway and actually bit his lip. God, it was sexy.

"Fuuuck," Valen groaned as he looked me over. "I want to rip that right off you, love."

I scoffed. "Why? Because it makes me look stupid?"

"Because it makes me want to lick every single inch of you."

I looked him up and down and could totally understand the sentiment. "Have someone bring us something more comfortable to change into, and you can get this off me however you like once we're done with your dad," I promised him.

"Done."

I smiled as he wrapped an arm around me and pressed a kiss to my lips before we headed for Dad's room. Cillian, Neo, Valya, and Apollo were already there. The latter three simply as witnesses and in case things went south.

"Harlow—" Cillian started when he saw me.

"Don't 'Harlow' me, Cillian," I snapped, and I saw the respect in his eyes. "I'm here to tell you that I *will* be marrying Valen, and you can consider that recompense for the betrayal and attack on me by Kane." Cillian opened his mouth to argue, and I shook my head. "Oh, no," I huffed a humourless laugh. "Sorry, no. This isn't a negotiation, Kincaid. You can either agree, or I will systematically stomp your empire to less than dust beneath the heel of my Louboutin's."

Cillian looked at me for one. Two. Three very pregnant heart beats. Finally, he turned to Valen. "I see why you love her." His eyes came back to me, and he inclined his head. "You have my permission, my agreement and, for what it's worth, Miss Vanguard, my blessing to marry Valen."

I was a little bit surprised that he'd folded that easily. I wondered if I'd really impressed him that much, or whether it was more a sign of how badly he felt about Kane.

"I will take nothing short of a full agreement to the terms set out in the contract as well as your assurance that the Kincaids will hunt down every single remaining member of the Black

Bloods and make them wish they'd never been born."

Cillian crossed his arms as he looked me up and down. "The Kincaids do not hesitate to go to war for their own, daughter. Believe me when I say that the Black Bloods will pay for what happened to you, for letting my idiot progeny lead them, and for their betrayal against the Company."

When no one said anything, I looked around. "Is that… Is that it?"

Cillian laughed and I had to wonder how I ever really found him that intimidating. "Now we double check the fine print, we haggle over the minute details like who gets the odd and even Christmases, if we'll call the children Kincaid or Vanguard, and sign the damn thing."

All this time and uncertainty and…that was it? I chuckled, feeling a sense of nervous disbelief, but everyone else in the room was smiling.

"But…" I started. "But I was ready to fight."

"You did fight," Cillian assured me. "Every day to this point. The first time we met. Every email. Every point in this very specific contract. Last night. The moment you put on that dress and walked into this room to keep fighting. I'd say you had the heart of a Kincaid if that didn't do a disservice to your father."

"Much appreciated, Cillian," Dad said, a slight note of warning in his voice, but there was enough warmth in it that I realised just how different this contract was to the one Archer had forced our family into.

The day Archer and Dad announced my future union with Apollo, Dad's eyes had been tight, there had been no smiles.

He'd sipped the drinks Archer poured him as slowly as possible to avoid imbibing more than strictly necessary.

Now, I watched as Dad poured everyone a shot and passed them out before clinking his glass with Cillian's, shouting 'slàinte mhath' at the top of their lungs and throwing their drinks back.

"Is this what every deal is like?" I asked.

"Every good deal, aye," Valen answered as he tipped back his glass.

I looked at mine and figured one would probably not make me give up any of the clauses I had painstakingly made sure to add to the contract.

But, of course, it wasn't just one. Our dads had emptied a whole bottle before we actually sat down to go over the details of the contract. Let alone sign anything. Valen and Apollo had been responsible for a few glasses each. I'd stuck with one. Valya had made impressive progress on a bottle of vodka. And Neo had abstained.

"Do we need a date by which the marriage needs to take place?" Cillian asked.

Dad frowned. "You think the Council will be more likely to accept it if we make it more of a business deal?"

"I'm wondering if it hurts. We can always set it far enough that the young 'uns would choose to be married by then anyway."

Now that I'd won Cillian over, the dads seemed quite happy to nut out the details for us. Or maybe it was a combination of excitement and alcohol.

Dad nodded, then surprised me with his next words.

"Harlow wants to be married in Scotland. I'm assuming this won't be a problem."

I wasn't sure why my eyes darted to Apollo there. Probably because of our conversation that seemed so long ago now. About where *we'd* get married.

Cillian scoffed. "Och, aye," he affected an exaggerated accent. "Why would we be okay with that, then?"

"At Balling Keep," Dad clarified.

For a moment, Cillian hesitated, all humour dropped. "Balling Keep?"

Dad nodded. "My wife's family's property."

"Aye, I ken Balling Keep, Vanguard, ye walloper." Cillian looked at me. "It would be an honour for my kin to be married at Balling Keep."

I wanted to know what the significance of Balling Keep was to Cillian and his kin but decided that that would be something I could talk to Mum about herself as soon as I told her that we were going to get the wedding we'd always wanted. God, she was going to be almost as excited as I was.

There were a few more details to sort out, a few more bottles to empty, plenty of food to enjoy, and finally a contract agreed upon and signed by all relevant parties. Considering how much alcohol the dads had been putting away, they were both still very with it.

"How soon can we call summit?" Cillian asked.

Dad scrubbed a hand over his chin. "If we cash in on Kane's actions last night, I think we could get them to convene as early as Tuesday."

"You're not going to tell them?" Cillian seemed surprised.

Dad shook his head. "The real reason we want to meet them? No. That will give Archer time to mount a defence. I got to them and claim that we can't reach terms for reparation and need them to mediate. We're both sitting members so the whole Council will be forced to convene. We enter and Harlow hits them with her intention to marry Valen."

Cillian was grinning. "I think we can make that work, Vanguard."

CHAPTER EIGHTEEN

As we stood in the elevator, waiting for it to take us to our floor, Valen's hand caressed my stomach gently. My whole body tingled, and I knew where we'd both rather he put his hands, but Valya and Neo were in the elevator with us.

"Is anyone else feeling incredibly horny all of a sudden?" Apollo teased. He sniffed dramatically. "Like it is on the air or something. Infectious."

Neo cleared his throat awkwardly, which only made the rest of us smile harder.

"They deserve to celebrate their win," Valya said.

"Is that the difference with sisters?" Apollo asked.

"What?" Valya answered.

"Sisters want to get you laid, and brothers will kill anyone who touches you."

"Speaking from your *extended* experience, mate?" Valen teased and I grinned.

"That's my experience of my found family," I interjected. "Florence was very willing to risk the wrath of the big, bad wolf to go behind your back and get me laid. You on the other hand—"

"Saw red at the thought of anyone else touching you," he growled, his nose dipping to my ear.

I opened my mouth to reply, but the doors opened. Neo cleared his throat again and inclined his head to us. "If I don't see you before you leave…" He inclined his head as though Valen would know the rest of the sentence.

Valen's arms wrapped around my front, and I felt him nod. "Ta, brother."

"I'll see ye on the other side," he directed to me, "and be proud to call you sister, Harlow."

"Thank you, Neo. And thank you for…just everything."

"Kincaids go to war for the Family." He swept out of the elevator, his eyes avoiding Valya in what I thought was a quite pointed way.

When the doors closed, Valen smacked his sister gently. "Do ye have to stir him?"

Apollo sniggered.

She smiled and it was all feline. "Perhaps he should not make it so easy, *nyet*?"

"*Nyet*," Valen huffed, wrapping me up tighter.

"Now, I will get to call you sister as well, *da*?" Valya said to me.

I nodded. "It looks that way."

She nodded. "Babushka will be pleased. I told her of you, Harlow Vanguard, and she cannot wait to meet you."

I felt Valen's smile drop. "Meet, when?" he asked.

Valya smirked as the elevator doors opened on our floor. "The Russians are coming, brother. Are you prepared?"

"No," he wheezed as she clapped him on the back.

"Oh, shit," Apollo chuckled.

I slid out of Valen's arms, took his hand, and tugged him to follow me. It didn't take a lot of convincing.

"We will speak soon, *sem'ya*," Valya said as the door closed on them behind us.

"Why in the fuck are the Russians coming?" Valen breathed as we walked to our room.

"Can I propose a counter question?" I asked him.

"I'm open to suggestions," he said.

"Exactly how did you want to get this dress off me, then?"

He spun us and pressed me against the wall to kiss me hard. His hand dropped to my leg, and he gathered my skirt up in his fist until he could press his hand against my bare thigh and grip it tightly. My arms wound around his neck as our bodies ground together. Valen's lips trailed over my cheek and down my neck, and his teeth grazed over my skin hard enough for the sting to ricochet to my clit.

Smiling, I pushed him away only enough to coax him to our room. He refused to take his lips off mine for longer than necessary and we almost fell through the door when we finally got to it and got it open.

As he kicked the door closed behind us, he grabbed the neckline of my dress and quite literally ripped it off my body. I gasped in shock as I looked at him. His eyebrows bounced as he looked at me through his hair and a very sinfully cocky half-smile tugged at his gorgeous lips.

"You said anyway I wanted, love," he reminded me.

"I know I did, and I'm not sure why I'm surprised that's the method you chose."

He picked me up and carried me to the bed as he peppered me with kisses. "We might have forever now, love, but that doesn't suddenly make me a patient man."

I wrapped my arms around him. "Good. Because I want you, Valen."

He growled appreciatively as he lay me on the bed. "Have I told you that you might be the death of me?"

I shrugged, all coy. "Maybe once or twice."

He shook his head as he ripped his open and pulled it off his arms. "Just once or twice?"

I sat up and undid his belt for him. He stood at the foot of the bed, and it was actually quite a convenient height for mouth.

"What are you planning here, love?" he asked, his tone cheeky.

"Let's see you comes undone first," I told him before I took his cock out of his trousers and ran my tongue over it.

He let me pleasure him until he started throbbing between my lips, then he dropped down and buried his head between my legs.

Without the worry of being caught or hiding behind disdain for each other, we went out of our way to take our time with each other in a way we'd only really ever done once; the night we were supposed to be fucking each other out of our systems. Lips hovered and explored as much as hands. We just lay together, sometimes talking, sometimes just relishing in the company without it needing to be anything more than just the two of us together.

"I don't have to anything to give you tonight, love," he said softly, as though he was thinking about that night as well.

My hand went to his cross at my neck as I looked to his wrist and saw my chain still peeking out from under his cuff. "Yes, you have," I told him, rolling over to lay my chin on his chest.

His eyes flashed wicked mischief. "Are you already thinking about those kids, love?" he teased.

I smiled. "Not...yet. But later, because what you've given me, Valen, is a future. A life. I know we still have to go before the Council and that's really scary, but we've got this far together."

He cupped my cheek in his hand. "We can get through anything else together as well."

I leant up and kissed him softly. It was a kiss without any real end. A kiss that continued until he was hard again and right on through until he was done again, and even then, a little bit longer still.

† † † †

We didn't hear back about the summit until the next day.

"The emergency summit is set for tomorrow. We'll go straight from here to the Council chambers," Dad said. "That will give us time to prepare and be well rested."

"Where are the Council chambers?" I asked.

Valen's jaw was tight. "Prague."

I nodded. "And who's coming?"

Dad looked around. "Only the four of us will be in the chambers for the summit. With Marco and Fender...indisposed, we'll take Apollo and Kieran with us. Cillian and Valk with have Neo and, I assume, your sister?"

Valen nodded. "Considering he ignored her for over twenty

years, Da has taken quite the shine to her.”

“Which is more than can be said for your brother,” I commented dryly.

Dad smirked. “I imagine he finds it difficult to know what to do with her.”

“Kincaid men *are* well known for confusing the urge to fight and fuck,” Valen admitted, and I choked on my own spit.

“What have I said about boundaries?” I spluttered.

“And what have I said about honesty?” Valen countered and I glared at him.

“I’ll make sure you have everything you might need waiting for you in Prague when we get there,” Dad said, trying and failing to hide his smile. “Is there anything you want to do before we leave, or will I call and make sure the jet is ready?”

“Can I see them?” I asked.

Valen took my hand and squeezed it.

“They’re still induced,” Dad told me, and I nodded.

“I know, but… I need to see them.”

“Then you’ll see them. Take two hours. That will still get us to Prague before dinner. Plenty of time to rest before the summit tomorrow.”

I gave him a hug and he returned it ten-fold. “Thanks, Dad.”

“Of course, darling. Anything for the woman calling the shots, you know that.”

I pressed a kiss to his cheek and his arms tightened before he let me go.

“Take the others. I’m not willing to take any risks.”

“What about you?”

“I’ll have Kieran and we’re not planning on going

anywhere."

"Neo will stay with Da, but Apollo will want to come and Valya might prove useful," Valen said.

We collected Apollo and Valya and spent a rather quiet ride to the hospital in Valen's Viper. I sat in the front with Valen, and the others were in the back. I wondered if Apollo felt as guilty as I did over Fender and Marco. Did he feel responsible? Did he think it was my fault? I wouldn't have blamed him if he did.

I took Valen's hand as we walked through the hospital to their room, glad that my injuries had been superficial enough not to need more than some salve and dressings. Machines beeped, that sterile smell crawled up my nose, and the lights were very bright.

But my discomfort meant nothing as we got to the door, and I saw Marco and Fender lying in their beds. They each had their own machines that beeped, connected to them with tubes and wires. Valen's hand tightened in mine and Apollo swore behind me.

"This fucking shit."

I hesitated, then took a few steps into the room, inadvertently dragging Valen with me with our hands still clasped.

Both of my Angels had bruising and cuts. Marco's arm was in a cast and Fender had one on his leg. Their chests rose and fell in time with the machines' beeping and there was something very unnatural and robotic about them. My heart twinged in my chest and a part of me regretted demanding that we come. Seeing them like that, I had trouble picturing them whole and healthy again. But I knew I would have felt worse had I not seen them.

I pulled up a chair and sat by them for five or ten minutes, but there really wasn't much else any of us could do. So, eventually we left them to heal and made our way to the airport to meet Dad and Kieran for our flight to Prague.

Chapter Nineteen

I walked into the Council chambers with Dad at my back. It was just us. After all, there were protocols and pretences here that we had to follow if we wanted to make sure this worked. We'd come too far to fuck it up now.

My feet stalled as I walked into their chambers. Geez, but they took this whole thing old school. The Council were seated up behind a raised bench like you saw judges sitting at. The room was circular and there were two tables in front of the bench. Valen and Cillian stood at one table as Dad directed me to the other. Valen, playing his part well, didn't turn despite the way my heels clacked on the floor unmistakably.

I looked up at the Council. There were two empty seats up there: Dad's and Cillian's. There was Archer and ten others. All men. Unsurprisingly. I recognised Marco's dad, but none of the others for sure. They were dads of people I'd been to school with, but that was as far as I knew them.

"Harlow Vanguard," the one in the very middle said as Dad and I took our place behind our table. "You have come before the Nameless on a matter of grave urgency."

I swallowed hard and nodded. "I have."

"Then state your business, girl," another sneered.

Archer kept shooting looks to Valen and Cillian, and I knew he'd bought our story.

"I come before the Council of the Nameless to proclaim my intention to marry Valen Kincaid."

A great furore exploded among the bench. The most vocal of them was Archer, as expected. After all, we'd told the Council that we were here to demand reparations for Kane's attack on me. They were expecting us to be against the Kincaids, not with.

"You what?" the Council leader asked.

I licked my lip and held myself as tall as I could. "I'm going to marry Valen Kincaid." I nodded towards him as though they might have forgotten who I was talking about.

"You are engaged to marry Apollo," Archer snarled.

I shrugged. "I'm pretending to be engaged to Apollo," I clarified.

Honestly, I was terrified. These men were looking at me like I was less than something gross on the bottom of their overly expensive shoes. They could crush me. Literally and figuratively. And Archer's face was twisted in furious retribution at my pronouncement. But I'd mastered masks in my eighteen years in this world. I'd suffered at the hands of the Black Bloods and Kane. I'd fucking raced up the mountain in Valen's precious Viper. If I couldn't stand up there now and act like I owned the whole lot of the miserable misogynists, then I didn't deserve anything I was fighting for.

"Explain yourself," the Council leader said over the hubbub that had erupted at my words.

"As my father's heir, I have negotiated a contract with Cillian Kincaid for his son Valen's hand in marriage."

Their outrage was almost deafening, but I held my own, staring up at each of them in turn.

"To what end?" the Council leader asked.

"Legion!" Archer cried, standing up and pointing at me. "They're trying to break the Law of Legions. They're planning to take over the Council and the Nameless for themselves."

If I didn't know Archer was about to get his comeuppance, I'd have felt something more than amusement at the victory on his face. He honestly thought he had me – us – here. Did he still think I was so irrelevant that I hadn't covered all these bases?

"Well?" the leader said. "What say you to these claims, Miss Vanguard, because they have legitimacy in my eyes."

I tried not to look too cocky. "I counter that Archer Callahan had a far worse violation planned." I turned to Dad, and he passed me the folder we'd prepared. I held it up so the Council would see it. "These papers prove that Archer Callahan was planning a permanent joining of the Callahan and Vanguard empires, compared to the temporary alliance we are proposing between the Vanguard and Kincaid families, one which would only last for the lifetime of our marriage."

The Council leader opened his mouth to interject, and I frowned at him before continuing loudly enough that, if he did interrupt, he'd be drowned out, "The contract between the Vanguards and Kincaids is a necessary bypass of the Law of Legions due to the threats Archer Callahan has made not only against *my* life but also my father and his business. If you look over these, you will find the proof that Archer Callahan was intending to assimilate the Vanguard empire into the Callahan empire on his way to actually monopolising the Company. The contract I am here to bring before you today is an agreement to marry Valen and I in exchange for an exclusive contract, but allows the Vanguard and Kincaid businesses to exist separately with no intention to merge them or their funds."

The Council leader looked like he was willing to hear me out, despite Archer's protests. I suspected that the only reason Archer was silent at this point was because he knew I had the proof in my hands. He knew we'd cornered him, and he was undoubtedly trying to come up with a way to spin the whole thing to his advantage. Or just get out of it as less scathed as possible.

"Bring me the documents," the leader said.

Someone rushed out of the shadows, took it from me and passed it to the leader. He opened the folder and started scanning them. It didn't take him long to realise that what we had was legitimate.

"Archer, explain yourself," he finally said, turning the might of his fury on Archer. He pointed to the page in front of him. "Because these tell me that you're planning not only to betray a sitting member of the Council of the Nameless, but also the Council as a whole."

"I saved his life!" Archer spat.

"A life debt does not negate the Law of Legions, Archer."

I cleared my throat and they all looked at me. "I also think you'll find that Archer set up my father's life to hang the debt over him and then started a turf war with the Rossanos when he didn't hold up his end of the bargain."

The council leader actually looked exasperated at this point. "You did, what?" he asked Archer. "That was what that was about? You brought that on yourself and then demanded the Council intervene?"

Archer stammered for a moment, and I was gratified to see him the most awkward and uncertain as I had ever seen him. "I… I am still a sitting member of this Council," seemed to be his only defence.

The Council leader looked to Cillian. "And the Kincaids have signed this contract under no duress?"

"The Kincaids are more than happy to sign Valen over to the Vanguards," he said with a nod.

The Councilman's eyebrow rose as though he wasn't expecting that response.

Cillian smirked, big and wide and actually really warm. "My son's gone and lose his heart, Lincoln. And Miss Vanguard has more than proven herself worthy of taking on a Kincaid. I would be proud to call her my daughter."

Valen did shoot me a look here and I saw the pride in his eyes that I'd not only won his father over but, in doing so, secured Cillian's approval of the contract. I knew Cillian also felt somewhat guilty over Kane's actions, but I liked to think that it was mostly me.

"And this business with Kane and the Black Bloods?" the council leader asked, like his mind was on the same path as mine.

Cillian nodded. "Had some bearing on my decision," he admitted. "I felt like I owed Miss Vanguard something, and giving her the contract she clearly deserved seemed fair compensation."

The councilman, Lincoln, nodded, looking down at the papers in front of him again. "So, the contract between Callahan and Vanguard was coerced. The contract between Vanguard and Kincaid was not only peaceably negotiated, but is also a… Did I hear right that it is a matter of the heart?"

I mean, we hadn't been going to bring that up if we didn't have to. But now that it was out there.

"You mean, this filth seduced my son's fiancée?" Archer spat.

"If I were you," Cillian said carefully. "I'd keep my fucking mouth shut, Archer."

"I am inclined to agree until I have all the facts," Lincoln said. He looked at me. "You love Valen, Miss Vanguard."

I nodded. "Yes."

He looked at Valen. "And you, Valk?"

Valen nodded. "I love her."

"And Apollo?" Lincoln asked, looking between me and Valen as though wondering which of us would answer.

Knowing I was supposed to be at the helm, Valen kept quiet. But before I could speak, Cillian was the one who answered, "Archer's young pup was instrumental in cementing the new contract. He had championed this relationship since Rex first came to me to open negotiations."

"Apollo sides with me," I agreed, ignoring Archer's fury.

"Well," Lincoln said slowly, not hiding his surprise quickly enough. "It seems we need to deliberate."

"What?" Archer yelled. "You cannot be serious? If you let this contract stand, then they could all turn around and take over the whole Company. The life of their marriage? It would take them mere months to depose the lot of us."

"And I suppose you pulled that number out of thin air, Archer?" I asked. "It's not like you've spent the last ten years planning it or anything."

I felt Dad's supressed amusement behind me.

"The Council will retire and make their decision. Naturally, Kincaid, Vanguard and Callahan will recuse themselves. We will let you know when we have reached our decision."

Dad's hand brushed mine, reminding me to wait until the Council had walked out. Archer threw us a look, but he was heavily encouraged to leave with the others.

It wasn't until the door clanged shut behind them that I felt like the four of us left in the room let out a breath.

"That could have gone worse," Cillian said to Dad as Valen came over to me and wrapped his arms around me. Cillian laughed. "Lord, boy. If I didn't love you so much, I'd be disgusted by this display of emotion."

Valen turned to his father with a steely glare. "If I didn't love you so much, I'd put you down for the insult."

"Just so long as you're not having second thoughts."

"Does it look like they're having second thoughts?" Dad said with a smirk.

I flushed. There was something about trying to have and express a grown up and mature relationship while your dads were teasing you that was making it very difficult. But then, I supposed that they'd do this whether we were eighteen or fifty. Dads would be dads, after all.

"How long do ye think they'll take?" Cillian said.

Dad scrubbed a hand through his hair. "Difficult to say. We've handed them some pretty damning evidence. Without Archer there to argue his way out of it, it should be pretty quick."

"I don't like a deliberation of ten, Vanguard. We're an odd number for a reason."

Dad nodded. "The Branches might side with Archer, but they know Apollo has more say in appointing his successor. If they want to crown Tyson God, they'll vote for us."

"If they left us here, they mustn't have planned to be long," I said, and Dad nodded.

"Lincoln will see this as pretty open and shut."

Cillian seemed to agree. "He's hated Archer for years. This is his chance to rip as much of Callahan's power out from under him as possible."

I took Valen's hand for comfort. "What does that mean for Apollo?"

Dad shrugged. "Depends on how Archer takes whatever the Council decide for punishment."

"If they're smart, they'll just induct the whelp as the head of the Family and give him his father's seat on the Council," Cillian scoffed.

Dad inclined his head. "If they're smart. Lincoln might be worried that gives this alliance too much power for now, though."

"Aye, that he might."

"Why?" I asked.

"Because any idiot knows that if the boy's given up his fiancée to his best friend and championed them to the detriment of his own father and name, then he's in yer pocket, Harlow. Lincoln might be in a rush to allow our contract, but he's not going to give us three seats on Council."

I shook my head. "I still have so much to learn."

Dad put his hand on my shoulder. "And there's plenty of time."

"Aye," Cillian agreed. "You purported yerself with grace, dignity and poise today, Harlow. Any member of the Company will see yer worth after this. Ye'll have made allies today that may not show their cards for many years, but they'll be there. In the shadows."

"There will be plenty who want to see her and the whole Vanguard empire in ruins because of it as well," Valen muttered.

Dad nodded. "They will. If the Council rules in our favour, though, then we'll be virtually untouchable."

The dads' talk turned incidentally to business, so Valen and I sat at one of the table's together, hands clasped and pretending we weren't both horribly nervous. Neither of us said anything and I think there was far too much to say and no knowing what needed to be said first. What if we lost? What if we won?

† † † †

"Has the Council come to a decision?" Dad asked when they trooped back in.

"They have," one of the council members answered as the ten of them took their seats; Archer was missing.

"We have gone over all the provided documentation and reached a decision. Valen Kincaid will marry Harlow

Vanguard," was Lincoln's pronouncement. "But there will be no exclusive contract. If this is, as you would claim, a love match then that is all it will be. The Kincaid family will remain available to any who can afford their services. Outside the usual standard of contracts, Valen alone will be beholden to his wife's family, and it will be up to the Kincaids whether he still works for them or not. Any child or children of their union can stand to inherit from Vanguard, Kincaid or Volkov lines, dependent upon each line's choosing. We will, however, allow the Kincaid Family to enact revenge on the Black Bloods for the grievances towards Miss Vanguard in whatever manner they see fit.

"Further, the Council of the Nameless decrees there will be no retaliation or recompense for the broken marriage contract between Vanguard and Callahan, as punishment for Callahan's actions to date. Harlow Vanguard is officially recognised by the Council of the Nameless to be the heir to the Vanguard empire and this verdict is only able to be changed by the last will and testament of Reginald Vanguard. Archer Callahan is henceforth on probation until such time as he proves himself loyal to the laws that bind us once more. His seat on the Council will remain open until the next elections."

"So, the Council have ruled," one of the other councilmen said.

"Next time we see you come before us, Harlow Vanguard," Lincoln said to me, "make sure it is to take your rightful seat beside us. I only hope I am still alive to see it."

I nodded, feeling my heart swell. "I will."

Dad looked over to me and inclined his head once.

"Then this session of the Council is done. You are dismissed. Enjoy your lives," were Lincoln's parting words.

Valen squeezed my hand, and we followed our father's out of the chamber.

"Well," Cillian boomed as we congregated in the lobby. "Aren't I glad we spent all that time drafting up a contract only to have them come along and write us a whole new one?"

Dad smiled. "We had to give them something to do."

Cillian laughed. "That we did, Vanguard." He held his hand out to Dad. "To joining our families, Rex."

Dad shook his hand, both of them smiling at each other with genuine warmth. "To joining our families, Cillian." They started walking towards the door together. "I suppose we should think about having you and the family over for dinner sometime. I would very much like to talk to Valya some more."

"You just tell us when and we'll be there. Is Sissy still doing that roast…?"

"Fuck," Valen murmured to me as the dads kept talking.

"What?" I laughed.

"I didn't think about that."

"About what?"

"About…family stuff. Like…family dinners." He actually shivered like the idea was heinous to him and I bit my lip uncertainly. He cleared his throat. "It's not that I don't want to. We just… Well, let's just say, the Vanguards do Christmas very differently to the Kincaids."

"I would actually pay to see our dads have a drink off."

The corner of his lips tipped. "You know what? So would I."

He put his arm around my shoulder as we headed for the car. Cillian insisted on taking us all out to dinner before letting Valen and I head back to school.

Chapter Twenty

When we got back to school, there was no reason for me to be wearing Apollo's ring anymore. I gave it back to him, noting the small note of regret in his eyes despite the wide smile at his lips, and slipped Valen's simple cross ring on in its place.

There was also no reason to pretend Apollo and I were anything other than good friends. The children of the Nameless didn't seem surprised and I was sure that the rumours had run rife since I'd appeared before the Council. Those who weren't directly affiliated with the Nameless were understandably confused that I was suddenly walking through campus holding Valen's hand while laughing with Apollo.

But, with Apollo's obvious blessing, there was nothing anyone could or would say or do. God had decreed that the newly crowned Goddess of Saint Benedicts was dating the Big Bad Wolf.

On that first day back, I noticed Sister Agnes look at Valen's ring on my finger. She gave me one single nod, but I understood her thoughts well enough. They were loud and clear in her eyes; she was both proud and impressed. It seemed that whatever relationship the nuns of Saint Benedicts had with the Nameless, they heard all the rumours as well.

Walking through school with Valen, just living our lives like we were boring and normal, took some getting used to but it also felt like the most natural thing in the world. I simultaneously felt like everything was finally right, but also like we were doing something naughty after so long having to hide our relationship.

We walked to breakfast a week later, Valen's arm around my shoulders as Apollo and Florence discussed something from either side of us. Apollo laughing in his surety and Florence vehemently disagreeing, their bickering was nothing Valen and I hadn't dealt with a million times before. Well, me more than Valen.

He dipped his lips to my temple for a kiss as he manoeuvred to open the door for us.

"Thanks, love," I said to him, slipping my hand into his so we could merge to single file to more easily get around people.

They parted for us the same way they would have a year ago. Their eyes lingered no longer. They whispered no more words. For all intents and purposes, everything was fine and normal. The stark reality, though, was that we had changed the way the Saints worked. We – Valen and Apollo – ignored the Magdalens, leaving the younger Saints and Saintlings to squabble among themselves to find their new normal.

The end of the school year was swiftly coming for us. Exams and final assignments were finishing up. But there was something so very lacking about it.

We'd started the year with a very firm hierarchy in place.

Four Angels shall there ever be to help uphold God's

sovereignty.

Come May, there was no God. There was a Goddess. And, while she had four serving Angels, two of them remained in hospital. But I'd faced Cillian Kincaid, I'd stood before the Council and won, and all the Saintlings knew it, even if they weren't supposed to.

No one dared mess with me. Even Ryko bowed his head to me whenever we passed, even on those circumstances I was alone. There might not have been a new world order in the halls of Saint Benedicts yet, but there was space for one to grow. Whether things returned to the usual patriarchal bullshit after we graduated would remain to be seen.

I would have preferred to hand the title over to a woman. Triss was my first choice, but her brother Tyson had received the same upbringing as Apollo; win God, be God, do not lose God.

"Are you sure?" I asked Triss and she nodded quickly.

"I'm not Goddess material. Maybe I could take over after Tyson graduates?"

Which was actually not a bad idea, and I had both Apollo and Valen at my back as I impressed upon Tyson how excellent an idea that would be. He promised to do everything in his power to get her ready, and I promised him that, if he didn't, I would return and remove him from his favourite appendage. For a moment, I thought I'd gone too far, but then I'd seen the resolve in Tyson's eyes, and I knew that I'd cemented myself among the ranks of those who were to be feared and respected.

Almost six weeks after my ordeal with Kane, we walked off the campus of Saint Benedicts for what was very likely the last time. Dorms were packed up. Five years' worth of lives crammed into boxes and suitcases. Furniture dismantled and thrown in the back of trucks. Walls painted and curtains pulled down.

Floss and I shed more than a few tears in that last week.

Not because we were leaving Saint Benedicts, but because we were leaving each other, no matter how temporarily. Our whole friendship had been in that dorm. Many of our best memories were within those grounds. Saying goodbye to Saint Benedicts made it very difficult to tell ourselves that we weren't saying goodbye to each other.

But we still had a whole Summer ahead of us and, a few months ago, we had planned to make the most of it.

Chapter Twenty-One

Now? Now, our last summer holidays together were to be spent sitting in the hospital. Not that there was anywhere else we'd rather be. At least until – if – they woke up.

Marco and Fender had been moved to a bigger, shared room and the rest of us had two couches and a couple of tables to accommodate us. The nurses had long since stopped trying to get us to stick to allotted visiting hours.

At the end of those summer months, Florence was off to Paris. Apollo would be beholden to his father's name in whatever capacity that took. We had no idea if Marco and Fender would wake up, let alone when. And Valen and I had a whole damned life ahead of us to work out what to do with. It was bittersweet that we couldn't share that time with two of our closest friends. It just plain sucked that they were missing out.

The boys were still induced, and it had been three months since the crash. They looked better, but there was something about their brains that needed more time to heal.

For the most part, *my* wounds were healed. Some of Kane's more creative designs looked like they were going to scar, but I could hope that they'd either fade in time or I'd work past the feelings of hopelessness and weakness that overcame me whenever I looked at them.

"Where are you guys going to live?" Apollo asked casually, the first one to fish for the next topic of conversation the way we'd all taken to doing.

"They've got time to think about that, surely?" Florence said.

Valen looked at me. "Do you *want* to live together? I mean, properly?"

"Not just spending every night together anyway?" I clarified with a smile, and he nodded. "Our own place?" He nodded again. I sighed as I thought about it. "Yes. Yeah. I think… I don't know how or where or what, but yes. I like that idea."

Valen looked like he was trying – very badly – to hide how happy my answer made him. "Right. Okay, then."

For the past few weeks, the four of us had rented an apartment near the hospital. It had made visiting easier and there was something nice about being together that made Marco and Fender's absences easier. Plus, no one outright asked, but I suspected that Apollo wanted to put off going home and facing his father for as long as possible after what had happened. None of us wanted him to go either. I'd always known that Apollo would be blamed for losing me, and I didn't know what Archer would do to him after he'd not only lost me but also helped me betray his father with the Council. I was trying to think of a way to avoid him having to return, but so far I hadn't come up with anything that he'd accept.

Dad was more than happy to delay my internship, such as it was, until after the Summer ended to give me more time with

Florence and I was really looking forward to spending that time with him. We had grown so much closer in the last four months. It turned out that he had an actual sense of humour and was as happy to be teased as to do the teasing.

"Where are you living when you get to Paris?" Apollo asked Florence.

"Why? Are you fishing for a couch to surf?" she teased.

He shrugged. "Maybe I am."

Florence's expression softened. "No one would blame you, you know."

He gave her a gentle smile. "I know. Thanks."

Valen frowned as he picked up his phone.

"Who is it?" Apollo asked.

"Kieran O'Malley…" Valen said as he answered it. "Valk."

We all watched him listen to whatever Marco's dad had to say. His face went ashen.

"What? When? Where?" Valen stood up quickly, knocking everything off the table beside him.

"What's happened?" Florence asked.

Valen shook his head, then said into the phone, "Slow the fuck down. Of course, she's with me. We're at the hospital." A pause. "No change. What about…?" Another pause. "Fuck. No. Where the fuck were you?" Valen blinked, his eyes darting almost guiltily to Marco's unconscious form for a moment. "We'll be there." He hung up and his eyes found mine. "Love, I'm so sorry." He started packing up, putting his holsters back on.

Apollo and I stood up.

I wouldn't believe it. It was like I knew, but also didn't know what he was apologising for. "What?"

Valen's eyes darted to Apollo. "Archer's gunning for your dad. Kieran called for backup. They don't know how much longer they can hold him off."

"Where are they?" Apollo asked.

"Docks."

"That's almost an hour away!" I cried.

Valen stalked to the door. "Not the way I drive, love."

"Go," Florence said, pushing me after the boys. "I'll be here."

I felt like my whole world was falling out from under me.

The three of us bundled into Valen's Viper and he tore out of the hospital carpark. Had I not been so worried about Dad, I might have made some quip about the fact that Valen must have been taking Fender's driving lessons. As it was, I could barely think it without my throat constricting. I couldn't lose Marco and Fender *and* Dad. I tried very hard not to think about it.

We got to the docks just as Archer was running for a car in a rain of bullets. Apollo was out of ours before Valen had brought it to a full stop, his gun trained unhesitatingly at his father. One shot. Two.

Archer looked back and I saw the sneer on his face. He got into the car unscathed. As it drove away, Apollo kept firing until the car was out of range, and he was out of bullets.

"FUCK!" he yelled.

"Valk!" I heard a voice and we all looked over to see Kieran waving us over. "Quickly."

We ran. We ran like I hadn't run in…probably my whole life.

Inside, Dad was lying in a pool of his own blood. I counted at least three bullet holes in him. My heart caught painfully in my chest and then tried climbing out of my throat. My eyes were hot and prickled uncomfortably.

"There's no time to get him help," Kieran said. "Moving him would just make him bleed out faster."

"Harlow," Dad wheezed as I dropped beside him.

"Dad," I sobbed.

"Shh," he tutted. "Shh. We don't have much time. Apollo?"

He dropped beside me. "Rex?"

"You've made me proud, son," Dad told him. "You chose your own path. Become your own man. Don't let anyone take that away from you."

Apollo shook his head. "No. No, sir. I won't."

"Valk."

"I'm here."

Dad nodded. "Look after her. I'm glad she has you, that you found each other. I know you'll love her and protect her. It would have been my honour to call you 'son' for real."

Valen's jaw clenched. "Thank you, Rex."

Dad finally looked to me and took my hand. "Harlow, darling. Know that I am so proud of you. I am so proud of the woman you have become, the woman you will continue to grow into, whatever paths you take. I love you so much and I am so sorry I won't be there for you."

"Daddy…" I cried. "No. Please don't go. Not now."

"I regret the years we wasted. That we didn't spend as a real family. Don't regret your years, Harlow."

I leant my face on his chest and his hand went to the back of my head tenderly. Blood was getting everywhere, but I did not give a single shit. "Please don't leave me now…" I whispered. "I need you."

When he said nothing more, I realised there was no movement under my cheek. Tears fell as I pressed my face to him as though I could force him to start breathing again through sheer will alone.

"Love…" Valen breathed, his hand going to my shoulder.

I shook my head. "No," I begged, another sob wracking my body. "No. It's not fair. Tell me it's a dream, Valen. Please. Tell me I get to wake up now and Marco and Fender and Dad are all going to be there and everything's going to be okay. I can't… I'm not ready for this."

"We're all behind you, Miss Vanguard," Keiran said, his voice thick like he was staving off tears himself. "Our service is yours now."

Another sob as the emotion of the sentiment was too much for my grief to handle just then.

Valen dropped beside me. "You're ready, love. You know you are."

"And anything you're not ready for, you have us. Me, Valk, everyone who works – worked – for your dad."

"Callahan–" Keiran started.

"Don't call me that," he said. "Please. That man is not my father."

"Apollo," Keiran amended. "By rights, there'll be a fucking massive bounty out on his life now. He's gone against Council decree. It's open season on Callahans now."

I looked up. "Your mum."

Apollo nodded. I saw his eyes were red, but otherwise he looked as stoic as usual. "We'll find a way to get her out. Won't we, Valk?"

"Of course, we fucking will."

"Mum will take you both in. You and Frenella are always welcome at our…" I paused and looked at Dad's body.

If he was dead, everything was now mine.

"Let's worry about that later, love," Valen said as he put his hands under my arms.

I let him help me up and leant on him for support.

"We should get back to Florence," I said. "Then get somewhere safe. Defendable. Can we move Marco and Fender?"

Valen wrapped me up tightly. "We'll work it out. We're not losing anyone else."

"Leave clean up to me, ma'am," Kieran said to me. "You let me know when you're ready for your first report and where to meet you."

I sniffed and I nodded to him. "Okay. Thank you."

"Thank you for caring for my boy."

My smile was watery and snotty, but it was sincere. "He makes it very easy."

I said my final goodbyes to Dad and let Apollo and Valen lead me back to the Viper.

As we drove back to the hospital – at a much more stately pace – I sighed. "Someone's going to have to tell my mum." Tears threatened again at just the thought.

Apollo squeezed my shoulder. "It doesn't have to be you."

I nodded. "Yes, it does."

Before I had too much time to think about it, I called her. I managed not to break down until after we'd hung up. I suspected she held out just that long as well.

Marco and Fender were taken off their induction medications the next day. They woke up within hours of each other. By the time they were both ready for a conversation, they knew something was wrong.

"What happened?" Marco asked.

I shook my head as the tears threatened to overwhelm me again. I felt like I'd spent the better part of the last eighteen hours crying. I was amazed I had any liquid left in me.

"Harlow's dad…" Apollo's voice was cracked and hoarse.

I knew he blamed himself but, more than that, I also knew he was uncertain about his future now. He had all-but declared open war against his own name. While he'd been following the decree of the Nameless and would suffer no retribution from them, Archer's retribution was guaranteed.

Marco sat up awkwardly. "When?"

Between the three of us, we eventually managed to explain what he and Fender and missed while they'd been out. We avoided some of the more difficult details and they knew better than to ask for them.

"Oh, missus," Marco sighed when we were done. "I failed you."

I gave a spluttery huff of laughter. "You didn't fail me, Marco."

He looked at me like I was an idiot. "Yes, I did. I couldn't keep you safe quite literally to save my life. And now, your da..."

I sniffed against even more tears. "It sucks. It all sucks. But I don't want to be sad forever."

"What do you want to be?" Fender asked.

"Angry. Archer Callahan is going to pay for the games he's played with my life. I'm going to put him six feet deep and then so far behind me that he'll never bother me and mine again."

"I have one request," Apollo said.

"What is it?"

"Let me be the one to kill him."

We faced off in front of each other for a moment. So many unsaid things between us. I knew he needed the closure. He needed the closure and he thought he had something to prove. To himself as much as to anyone else. So, of course, I nodded.

"Deal."

"Good," Marco said warmly. "Now, as much as we appreciate you lot essentially moving into the place, go the fuck home."

"We'll be here tomorrow," Fender added. "But until then, we all need to shower and get changed. Like seriously guys, it's starting to smell in here."

Despite the forced joviality before leaving, when we got home that night, we were all sombre. In our room, Valen dropped to his knees in front of me and hugged my legs tightly.

"Valen–" I started, running my hands through his hair.

He shook his head. "Just let me have forever, love," he begged.

MORNINGSTAR: Book 4: Valen's POV coming soon
BROKEN GOD: Book 5: Apollo's POV coming soon.
SINS & SAINTS: Book 6: Florence duet #1 coming soon.

tHE SinnERs OF St BEnEDicts

If you liked *Men & Monsters*, share the love and let me know! While the trilogy currently sits as a standalone, I've got ideas for a whole series of follow-ups, including Valen's and Apollo's POVs, a HEA for Florence, 'next gen' plotlines, as well as a sequel to the alternate endings.

Print Books

Print versions of the Sinners of Saint Benedicts duet will be available from Elizabeth Stevens' webstore. They come in three versions:

1) the original duet version with all endings
2) the Harlow trilogy version, which will be what the Main Timeline follows on from.
3) the Why Choose trilogy version, which will tie-in with a sequel for the three of them.

PRINCE OF THORNS

A New Adult darker, enemies-to-lovers, academy, romance. Get it here: https://books2read.com/u/bryaD7

From Elizabeth Stevens, writing as E.J. Knox, comes...
The bad boy willing to risk everything – even his life – to get the girl.

People call them the V.I.C.E.S. because they'll wring you for everything you are and leave you ruined. They are the Princes of Rosewood Hall, and no one says no to them. Until now.

Vaughn Saint. The racer. He dubbed the Prince of Thorns. Pretty as a rose, but one touch and he'll leave you bleeding.

He chases death on two wheels at least twice a week. Used to controlling powerful things between his thighs, nothing is more powerful than the lure of the pleasures he promises.

And he wants to give them all to me. Only problem? I'm the daughter of the leader of the Blood Roses. His leader. I'm off-limits. Dad wants me to walk away from all that, not get dragged down deeper into their hell, but Vaughn Saint threatens to take me to the very depths and still have me begging for more. Loving me will kill him.

Not loving me will destroy the both of us.

Reign

From Elizabeth Stevens, writing as E.J. Knox, comes…

A King. An Heir. And the unwilling pawn with the power to win or crush a Royal coup.

Beckett Maxwell reigns over Rivermont Academy with his loyal court: the Royals, their courtiers, their harem. He doesn't have time for a nobody like me: a scholarship student and daughter of faculty to boot. I'm the lowest of the low in a school full of highs.

One year everything's going fine. Enough. The next, I'm some pawn in a Royal power struggle. Well, I won't have it. They can bully me, they can torment me, they can make my life miserable. But I will not be used in one of their twisted games.

But when the fox is lurking at the door, sometimes the only safety is in the arms of the lion. Beckett might actually be the lesser evil in this case. And I can't deny there's something between us. Something I wish wasn't there.

The closer we get, the further he pushes me away, but something keeps pulling me back. When it comes to Beckett Maxwell, I'm a sucker for punishment.

But I'll only bear it so long. If Beckett wants his claim on me to stick, then he might need to choose between his crown and my heart.

Lords of Phoenix Hall

If you liked *Gods & Angels*, you might also enjoy E.J.'s next release, *the Lords of Phoenix Hall*. Also a New Adult superhero bully romance, it's described as 'Sky High' meets 'the Boys'.

At Phoenix Hall, even the heroes are villains.
In my world, there are three kinds of people.
Heroes. Villains. Plebs.

Heroes save the world.
Villains try to take over the world.
Plebs just try to get through Chemistry without losing their eyebrows.

I'm Ruby Raddish, pleb. The lowest of the low. The utterly powerless child of two of our most famous heroes. Or I was. Until I accidentally blow up Lord Hero himself after one too many bad jokes at my expense. Now the target on my back has just tripled.
No matter which way I turn, I can't win.

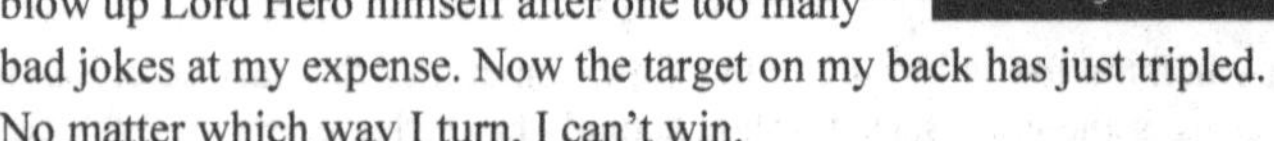
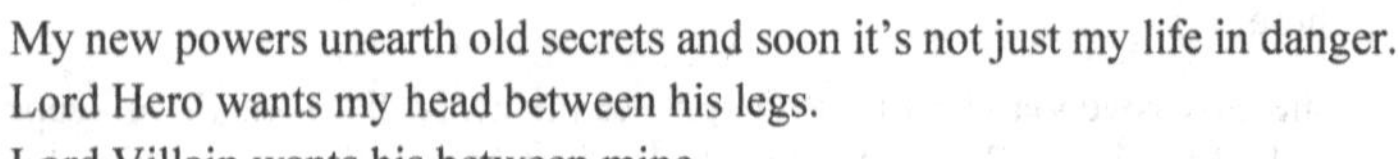

My new powers unearth old secrets and soon it's not just my life in danger.
Lord Hero wants my head between his legs.
Lord Villain wants his between mine.
I just want to graduate and disappear into the normalcy of a human life.

MEN & MONSTERS

Thank you so much for reading this story! Word of mouth is super valuable to authors. So, if you have a few moments to rate/review Harlow's story – or, even just pass it on to a friend – I would be really appreciative.

Have you looked for my books in store, or at your local or school library and can't find them? Just let your friendly staff member or librarian know that they can order copies directly from LightningSource/Ingram.

If you want to keep up to date with my new releases, rambles and writing progress, sign up to my newsletter at https://landing.mailerlite.com/webforms/landing/y1n6q2.

You can find the playlist for *the Sinners of Saint Benedicts* on Spotify:
I also have a generic writing playlist you can check out 😊

Follow me:

My Books

E.J.'s list is just getting started. While you wait for the next release, you can find where to buy all my books in print and eBook at the website; www.elizabethstevens.com.au/.

About the Author

E.J. Knox is the Darker/Bully Romance penname of Elizabeth Stevens. E.J. is the name to read if you want darker/bully romance in the Mature YA/NA crossover space. Think high school, college, and academy. E.J. brings my usual wit, banter, and repartee in good old enemies-to-lovers showdowns between alpha males and the sassy heroines strong enough to knock them down a peg or two. There'll be fake-dating, love triangles, kidnapping and danger, second chances, and more.

Writer. Reader. Perpetual student. Nerd.

Born in New Zealand to a Brit and an Australian, I am a writer with a passion for all things storytelling. I love reading, writing, TV and movies, gaming, and spending time with family and friends. I am an avid fan of British comedy, superheroes, and SuperWhoLock. I have too many favourite books, but I fell in love with reading after Isobelle Carmody's *Obernewtyn*. I am obsessed with all things mythological – my current focus being old-style Irish faeries. I live in Adelaide (South Australia) with my long-suffering husband, delirious dog, mad cat, two chickens, and a lazy turtle.

<u>Contact me:</u>
Email: ejknox@elizabethstevens.com.au
Website: www.elizabethstevens.com.au/ej-knox
Twitter: www.twitter.com/writer_iz
Instagram: www.instagram.com/writeriz
Facebook: https://www.facebook.com/elizabethstevens88/

www.ingramcontent.com/pod-product-compliance
Lightning Source LLC
Chambersburg PA
CBHW010555170726

48285CB00011B/2921